# London Diary:

Research. And that's a... [text obscured] ...

be breaking Rule 2—no men. I would simply be observing this man from a purely clinical point of view. My 'Living with a Playboy' idea would be like one of those fly-on-the-wall documentaries. I wouldn't be hands-on—I should be so lucky. More all hands to the pump—gulp—as I try to do my bit to save the agony aunt column. (Though I can't deny the thought of living so close to this particular playboy has done wonders for my metabolic rate. I've eaten a whole tub of double chocolate chip icecream in anticipation of his return and I can still get into my jeans...)

(Imagine how slim I'd be if we lived together permanently...)

(Not that I'd ever consider living with anyone after my experience with the ex....)

Love-life? Vicarious. Active. Very active indeed.

Lustful thoughts? Are there any other kind?

And the playboy? This might all be over by tomorrow. He didn't exactly seem thrilled to see me, and I have yet to discover how he feels when he returns from the gym to find I'm still here.

**Susan Stephens** was a professional singer before meeting her husband on the tiny Mediterranean island of Malta. In true Modern™ Romance style they met on Monday, became engaged on Friday, and were married three months after that. Almost thirty years and three children later, they are still in love. (Susan does not advise her children to return home one day with a similar story, as she may not take the news with the same fortitude as her own mother!)

Susan had written several non-fiction books when fate took a hand. At a charity costume ball there was an after-dinner auction. One of the lots, 'Spend a Day with an Author', had been donated by Mills & Boon® author Penny Jordan. Susan's husband bought this lot, and Penny was to become not just a great friend but a wonderful mentor, who encouraged Susan to write romance.

Susan loves her family, her pets, her friends, and her writing. She enjoys entertaining, travel, and going to the theatre. She reads, cooks, and plays the piano to relax, and can occasionally be found throwing herself off mountains on a pair of skis or galloping through the countryside. Visit Susan's website: www.susanstephens.net—she loves to hear from her readers all around the world!

**Recent titles by the same author:**

THE UNTAMED ARGENTINIAN
RUTHLESS BOSS, DREAM BABY

**Did you know these are also available as eBooks?**
**Visit www.millsandboon.co.uk**

# THE SHAMELESS LIFE OF RUIZ ACOSTA

BY
SUSAN STEPHENS

MILLS
BOON

All the characters in this book have no existence outside the imagination of the author, and have no relation whatsoever to anyone bearing the same name or names. They are not even distantly inspired by any individual known or unknown to the author, and all the incidents are pure invention.

First published in Great Britain 2012
by Mills & Boon, an imprint of Harlequin (UK) Limited.
Harlequin (UK) Limited, Eton House, 18-24 Paradise Road,
Richmond, Surrey TW9 1SR

© Susan Stephens 2012

ISBN: 978 0 263 89293 2

Harlequin (UK) policy is to use papers that are natural, renewable and recyclable products and made from wood grown in sustainable forests. The logging and manufacturing process conform to the legal environmental regulations of the country of origin.

Printed and bound in Spain
by Blackprint CPI, Barcelona

# THE SHAMELESS LIFE OF RUIZ ACOSTA

# PROLOGUE

STRETCHING out his powerful limbs, Ruiz Acosta took the call from his brother Nacho in Argentina. Gazing out across the sophisticated cityscape through the elegant window of his town house, Ruiz knew he had come to love London as much as the wild reaches of the pampas, if not more. The contrast was extreme and the challenges different, but just as stimulating.

And the women?

Pale, harried, and bundled up in so many clothes it was impossible to imagine them freeing themselves from the many wrappings long enough to make love—

'Will I be home in time for the annual polo match?' he asked, refocusing in order to reply to his older brother Nacho's question. 'Wild horses wouldn't keep me from that brawl. Just make sure I have a stallion that can out-run Nero's fire-breathing monster and I'll be back in time to watch your flank, Nacho—'

'And the business?' the hard male voice interrupted.

'We're in pretty good shape. I've completed the reor-ganisation. I just have to approve one or two new mem-bers of staff. I'll be splitting my time between Argentina and London in future, but—'

'So long as you don't forget your family on the other

side of the world, Ruiz,' Nacho interrupted. 'You're the glue that holds us together—'

'Glue can stretch,' Ruiz pointed out wryly.

Not liking this challenge to his authority, Nacho changed tack. 'Have you heard from Lucia, recently?'

'Lucia? No. Why?' Ruiz sat up, hearing the change in his brother's voice. 'Is there a problem?'

'Our sister's gone off radar again—changed her number—'

'Lucia was always tricky.' And who could blame her with four older brothers looking over her shoulder? Ruiz reflected. But his sister's safety was paramount. 'I'm on it. I'll drop by Lucia's flat later to see if she's back, or if she left any clues behind.'

Nacho seemed satisfied now he knew Ruiz was picking up the latest family problem; his voice mellowed into a dark-chocolate drawl. 'Have you found yourself a woman yet?'

Ruiz laughed as someone, or rather something, nuzzled its way between his knees. 'No, but a dog found me.' There was a curse on the other end of the line, which Ruiz ignored. 'This great black mutt wandered in from the street while I was having some furniture delivered and made himself comfortable in front of the fire. Didn't you, Bouncer?'

'You've given the dog a name?' Nacho interrupted sharply.

'Not just a name—a home. Bouncer is part of the furniture now.' Ruiz ruffled the big dog's ears.

'This is so typical of you, Ruiz,' Nacho rapped, reverting to elder brother mode. 'You always were a sucker for waifs and strays. If anyone needs TLC, you're there before they know they need help. *Dios!* Get rid of the mongrel!' Nacho thundered.

'Butt out!' Ruiz fired back. They weren't boys now for Nacho to push him around. His brother should know that where animals were concerned Ruiz cut no corners.

'See you at the polo match,' Nacho growled, 'without the mutt!'

'Goodbye to you too, brother,' Ruiz murmured, staring at the silent receiver in his hand.

Nacho had issues. Having taken responsibility for his siblings when their parents died, Nacho sometimes forgot they were all adults now and that, having made his home in London rather than the pampas, Ruiz was independently successful.

Sensing his irritation, Bouncer whined. He stroked the dog to reassure him. 'I should make allowances for Nacho?' Ruiz queried as Bouncer's expressive eyes invited him to take a walk. His brother ran an *estancia* in Argentina the size of a small country and Ruiz supposed Nacho was entitled to have his off days. 'Okay, boy, you're right. Let's go,' he said, standing up.

A big dog like Bouncer needed hours of exercise. Not unlike his master, Ruiz reflected, catching sight of his swarthy, unshaven face in the mirror. It had been another long and ultimately disappointing night. None of the women he'd met in London appealed to him with their bony figures, heavy make-up, and uniformly dyed blonde hair. It would be fair to say he had become more than a little jaded. Perhaps Nacho was right and he should return to Argentina to find some sophisticated, black-eyed siren, full of the fire and passion of South America who could not only match him in the bedroom but who would share his zest for life.

That was the type of woman his brother Nacho could do with, to shake him out of permanent warrior mode,

Ruiz reflected wryly as he locked the front door. It didn't occur to Ruiz that a similar wake-up call might be waiting for him just around the corner…

# CHAPTER ONE

*I've always kept a diary. I'm a compulsive writer
some might say. I've heard that in the absence of
anyone else to confide in people often record their
thoughts.*

*This is day one of my new life in London and my
train is just pulling into the station, so I have to
keep this short. To make sure everything is in line
with the K.I.S.S. principle—which, just in case my
journal is discovered a thousand years from now,
stands for Keep It Simple Stupid, there are only
two rules:*

*Rely on no one but yourself.*

*No men—at least, not until you are established as
a journalist and can call the shots!*

THERE was sleet dripping down her neck and a really old
man had just decided Holly was the one who needed help.
Was she trying to work out which bus would take her
to the station? 'No, but thank you for asking—I just got
here,' she explained. Chin up. Jaw firm. Smile big. Stop
tapping diary notes into your phone and put it away. 'I'm
waiting for a friend,' Holly added to reassure the elderly
Samaritan. Well, it was almost true. She was waiting to
get hold of a friend on the phone.

The old man wished her well and went on his way but with the brief moment of human contact snatched away again she felt doubly lost. It was the noise in London, the constant traffic and the mobs of people that took some getting used to when you had just arrived in the capital from a small market town. It didn't help that her winter coat was soaked right through, she was frozen, and her long red hair hung in sodden straggles down her back.

How could things go so wrong?

It wasn't as if she hadn't made the most meticulous plans before coming to London to take up the job at *ROCK!* magazine, carefully tallying her start date with an amazing offer from her best friend from school to stay in her central London garden flat until Holly could sort out her own accommodation. So how was it that the black cab that had brought her from the station to this faceless part of town had left her in front of a door that should have been flung wide in welcome but had instead been opened by a stranger who didn't even know her name?

Wiping the rain from her face, Holly pulled out her phone and tried to call her friend Lucia again.

'Lucia?' Holly exclaimed excitedly, forced to execute a little unplanned dance as she dodged spray from the traffic. 'Lucia— Can you hear me?' Holly yelled over a deafening soundtrack of horns tooting, grinding gears, and steel drums—

*Steel drums?*

'Holly!' Lucia shrieked with equal excitement. 'Is that really you?'

'Where are you, Lucia?'

'St Barts. Can't you hear the sea? Holly, it's incredible here. You'd love it—'

'St Barts in the Caribbean?' Holly interrupted, shivering as she bowed her head beneath a fresh onslaught of wind and icy sleet. Lucia was from a very wealthy Argentinian family, so anything was possible. 'Isn't it some unearthly hour there?'

'Dunno… Still partying!' Lucia shrieked as if to confirm this with a thousand friends.

'So…didn't you get my text?' Holly asked carefully.

'What text?' Lucia sounded bewildered.

'The one I wrote confirming I'd love to accept your invitation to stay with you this week until I find a place to live down here?'

'Breaking up…breaking up.' Lucia was shrieking with laughter now with her hand over the phone. 'This line is terrible, Holly,' she confided in a slurry voice. 'Why don't you just catch a plane and come over here?'

Er, zero cash? Zero bikinis? Zero desire to cop out of a life that had already been through the shredder…

Holly held back from explaining to Lucia that they might have attended the same school but, while Holly had been a full scholarship pupil, Lucia had been a new sports hall, an Olympic-sized swimming pool and a riding stables complete with indoor arena. Oh, yes, St Bede's School for Girls had had a very shrewd headmistress.

'So, where are you now, Holl?' Lucia demanded to the accompaniment of clinking glasses.

'Outside your flat. "Meet u apt 12/20th Nov",' Holly read the text from her phone, leaving out the bit about how Lucia 'cdnt wait', followed by ':-D' and a dozen exclamation marks.

'Did I send that?'

'Yes, but no problem,' Holly lied brightly.

Lucia groaned. 'I did! I said it would be okay for you to stay. I remember now. And it is okay. At least, it would be if I were there. And I sublet my part of the house. Oh, you poor darling, I completely forgot. Were they awful to you?'

'Actually—'

'But you can book into a hotel, right?' Lucia chirped before Holly could explain that the woman who had opened the door to her had been quite nice, if a little bewildered to find a stranger with a suitcase standing on her doorstep looking hopeful. 'Of course I can,' Holly soothed. 'I'm really sorry I interrupted your break, Luce—'

'No. Wait.'

'What?'

'The penthouse!'

'The penthouse?' Holly queried.

'The family's London penthouse is free! I'm sure it is.'

'The penthouse, where?' Holly said, frowning.

'Right there at the same address,' Lucia explained triumphantly. 'There's a spare key in the key box by the side door. Give me ten minutes to ring someone to make sure the penthouse is empty and find out what the code is.'

'Are you sure?'

'Is the sun shining in St Barts?' Lucia screamed with laughter. 'And there's a café right across the road,' she said. 'See it?' Lucia demanded, tense with excitement now she had identified a way out of the problem. 'Have a coffee and wait for me to call you—'

Holly stared at her silent phone. Only a member of the powerful Acosta clan could have a penthouse going spare in London, she thought wryly. Putting her phone away, she glanced across the road and saw the café Lucia had mentioned. The windows were all steamed up. It looked inviting, and also warm. But it also looked very smart,

Holly thought, losing confidence. The café was all black glass and bronze—the sort of place her boyfriend had frequented between those colossal deals he used to tell her he was brokering.

Her ex-boyfriend, Holly reminded herself as she started jiggling her cumbersome suitcase down the kerb. You didn't have to be middle-aged and weary to lose everything to a good-looking swindler, Holly had discovered. You could be young and ambitious, and think you knew it all too. But she wasn't going to let one mistake rule her life. She was going to forget Mr Crud-for-pants dipping his greedy little paws into her bank account, and start again. Right now her goal was reaching that café where she could have a hot drink and dry off while she waited for Lucia to call.

Choosing her moment, Holly launched herself across the road—only for her suitcase to get stuck at the opposite kerb long enough for a truck to drive past and soak her. She was still spluttering with shock when a huge black dog appeared out of nowhere and attempted to lick her dry. And now a hunk in jeans had joined the scrum. 'Here. Let me,' he insisted in a deep, husky voice with an intriguing accent. Lifting both dog and suitcase away, he tried to steer Holly off the road.

'Get off me!' She was spluttering with shock, her voice rising with each syllable as she attempted to push him away. But he was like a rock and what made it worse was that he was so incredibly good-looking—exotically dark, extremely clean, and very big—which made her feel correspondingly washed-out, mud-streaked, very clumsy, and annoyed.

'Sorry,' he exclaimed, turning away to comfort his over-excited dog.

'Can't you control your animal?' she flashed. 'Perhaps something smaller would be easier for you to handle?'

Holly's barb missed its mark by a mile. The man only seemed amused and succeeded in looking sexier than ever with his mouth pressed down as she ranted on. 'Bouncer is a rescue dog from the streets,' he explained, straightening up to his full, towering height. 'I still have to teach him manners. I hope you can find it in your heart to forgive him?'

The voice was as delicious as she had first thought, and she had stared for far too long into those dark, compelling eyes, Holly warned herself. But instead of standing on her dignity and ending this, she heard herself say, 'You could buy me a coffee and I'll think about it.'

'I could,' the man agreed.

Had she gone completely mad?

Was *Rule two: No men* out of the window already?

Hmm, maybe. The man was not only incredibly good-looking—tall, dark and handsome in the best possible way, which was to say a little rugged and not too contrived, with quite a thorough coating of sharp black stubble on his face and excellent teeth—but as well as an exotic accent he had an intriguing way of looking at her. His gaze didn't flicker away like some people she could mention, but remained steady on her face.

But was that a good enough reason to risk it?

'May I take your hesitation for acquiescence?' he prompted. 'You look frozen.'

She was. And the man's steady gaze was making her feel uncomfortable. She wasn't used to attracting interest from such good-looking men. Of course, it would have to happen when she looked more of a mess than usual. Typical. 'I suppose a coffee wouldn't hurt.'

'Strong, hot coffee is what you need,' he said firmly.

'But before we go inside, are you going to forgive my furry friend?'

How could she refuse a request like that? Her ex hadn't been able to get near a dog without it biting him, Holly remembered as the big dog stared back at her, panting hopefully. 'Forgiven,' she said, watching with interest as the man made a fuss of his dog, tempting him with a bowl of treats someone had laid out ready beneath the cafe's rain-proof canopy. He even pointed out the bowl of clean water—

'Bouncer's done a real number on your outfit,' he observed, turning round.

'Yes, he has,' Holly admitted ruefully. It wasn't so much an outfit as a motley collection of sale items she'd kept at the back of the wardrobe too long to take back to the store.

'How about I pay for dry-cleaning?'

'Oh, no. That's okay,' she insisted. 'The mud will wash off—'

'If you're sure? I'm happy to pay.'

A man offering to pay for anything was a first too, Holly thought. 'Really, I'm sure,' she said with a small smile, and then, embarrassed by so much concern and attention from a stranger, she turned away. 'Hey, Bouncer.' Predictably falling for the liquid brown sappy look, she started tickling the dog's ears, which Bouncer took as a cue to roll onto his back, waving his giant-sized paws in the air.

'You have a way with animals,' the man observed.

'When they're not trying to lick me to death,' Holly agreed wryly.

'Shall we?' he said, starting for the door.

In nothing more exciting than a pair of jeans, scuffed boots and a heavy jacket, he looked exactly like the type of man who could turn a girl's world upside down. Rebuilding herself after a devastating love affair meant stepping out and stepping up. It did not mean running away. And it was only a coffee.

The guy was so big he made Holly feel dainty as she walked past him, which was another first. She was built on a heroic scale, as her father always reminded her proudly before he gave her that second and rather concerned look—the one she was supposed to miss. But it wasn't every day a dog could coat her in mud and make her smile, or a man could hold her gaze for longer than two seconds. And at least he was polite, she reasoned as he held the door.

As the warm, coffee-scented air swept out to greet them Holly relaxed her guard enough to brush past him on the way in. The jolt to her senses woke her up and warned her to take more care in future. But it wasn't as if she was coming on to him, Holly reasoned. He was deeply tanned and film-star striking, while she was pale and not that interesting. But there was some common ground. She felt out of place in London and he looked about as much at home on a grey day in London as a polar bear on a beach—

And about as dangerous.

Once they were inside the café he reached behind the counter and grabbed a towel, which he tossed to her.

'Well caught,' he said as she gasped and snatched hold of the towel. 'May I suggest you wipe the worst of the mud off your clothes?'

'Won't they mind?' Holly said worriedly, throwing a guilty glance at the counter staff.

'They'll mind more if you don't wipe it off before you sit down,' the man observed, curving his attractive smile again.

Men as good-looking as he was could do as they liked, Holly concluded as she watched him return the towel with a few words of thanks to the staff. There wasn't one complaint. And why should there be? she thought as he shrugged off his jacket and everyone turned to look. Who wouldn't want a better view of that body? Holly mused as her gaze roved reluctantly past the well-packed jeans to the crisp white shirt with the sleeves rolled back to display a pair of massive forearms. Her day had definitely improved. Until the girls behind the counter started flirting with him and she felt a stab of something unexpected.

And a warning that drew a parallel between this man and her ex. The ex had been good-looking too, and had packed a certain degree of charisma—not pure, one hundred per cent gold star charisma like this man, but enough—until she had scratched the surface and found the base metal underneath—

'I'll get the coffee,' he said, distracting her, 'while you grab a table.'

She registered a shivery reflex when the man touched her shoulder and was powerless to hide the quiver of awareness that streaked through her. He must have felt it too. He had, Holly concluded, noticing how the steady gaze was now laced with humour. 'You might want to wipe some of the dirt off your backside before you sit down?' he murmured discreetly.

The fact that he'd noticed her backside was concerning. Craning her neck, Holly groaned.

'The ladies' room is just over there,' one of the waitresses supplied helpfully.

'Why don't you leave your suitcase with me?'

She looked at the man and evaluated her choices. She could leave her belongings with someone she didn't know, or struggle back through the crowded café with a large case in tow.

'You can trust me,' he said, reading her.

And you know what they say about people who tell you you can trust them, Holly thought.

'In my case it happens to be true,' he said evenly as if reading her mind were second nature to him.

She left the case.

Trying to ignore the amused glances of the up-market clientele, Holly retraced her steps through the café. As her face heated up under the critical scrutiny she realised that for the short time she'd been with him the man had made her feel good about herself. She didn't want to sit down in their fancy-pants café anyway. They probably charged twice as much here for a latte as they did at the popular chain down the road—

But rebuilding Holly meant never running away. And was she seriously going to make some pathetic excuse and leave an attractive man in the lurch?

Having cleaned herself up, she returned to find him reading the financial pages with her suitcase stowed safely at his feet. 'I had to guess what you'd like,' he said, setting the newspaper down.

'Skinny latte and a toasted cheese and tomato *ciabatta*? You're spoiling me—'

'No,' he said bluntly. 'I was ordering lunch, and I thought you might like some too.'

'Thank you.' An honest man was a refreshing change too. 'It looks delicious…?'

'Ruiz,' he supplied, reaching over the table to shake her hand.

'Holly.'

'Pleased to meet you, Holly.'

A lightning bolt shot up her arm when they shook

hands. And she shouldn't be staring at him like this. 'Ruiz?' she said. 'I love your name. It's so unusual.'

'My mother devoured romantic novels while she was pregnant. Mediterranean heroes?'

'I was born on Christmas day.'

They laughed.

And now it occurred to her that she couldn't remember the last time she had relaxed with a man. Laughing at the ex's jokes was expected, even demanded, but laughing because she was happy only brought accusations that she was braying like a donkey. So she didn't laugh.

'Is the coffee okay for you?' Ruiz said.

She looked at him. 'Delicious. Thank you.'

He held her gaze with eyes that were warm and interested. She wanted to know more about him. 'My guess is you're between seasons and that's why you're in London—'

'Between seasons?' Ruiz queried, frowning as he sat back. 'What do you mean by that?'

'Ski and surf? The tan, the build…' The confident swagger that came as standard equipment on a body when a man was in peak condition, she kept to herself.

'Am I so unusual?'

'Yes, you are.' Holly curbed her smile as Ruiz glanced around. He stood out like a very tanned and elegant thumb amongst a room full of stressed-out sore thumbs. 'But you've got a dog with you,' she said, frowning as she progressed her thoughts, 'so you must live close by.'

'Must I?' Ruiz queried with amusement. 'Do you always go into this sleuth-mode when you meet someone for the first time?'

'Sorry—it's really none of my business.'

'No harm done, Holly.'

She loved the way he said her name—and at least he

had remembered it—not that she was a troll, but if beauty was a matter of millimetres she could do with that extra inch.

Relaxing back in his seat, Ruiz tipped a toast towards her with his cup, which made Holly wonder if she was guilty of becoming too comfortable with a man she knew nothing about just because they were here in this safest of settings. The best thing to do was drink up and leave, she concluded.

'Hey, where's the fire?' Ruiz demanded as she gulped her coffee down.

How could anyone look so dangerous when they smiled? Ruiz's gaze was dark and experienced—with the emphasis on experienced. Heat curled deep inside her as he curved a sexy smile. 'I really should be going,' she said, coming to her senses. Why didn't her phone ring? What had happened to Lucia?

'Why the rush?'

'I thought you'd be pleased to be spared further investigation.'

'No, I like to hear your musings,' Ruiz argued. 'You've got a great imagination, Holly. Are you a creative, by any chance?'

'Advertising? No. I'm hoping to become a journalist,' she explained, though right now she wondered if she would make it to the first pay cheque. As far as interview technique went she was pants. She still didn't have a clue about Ruiz—where he came from, what he did—

'Do you have a job lined up?'

Holly brightened at the thought of it. 'Yes, I start as a lowly intern on *ROCK!* magazine on Monday—'

'*ROCK!* magazine.' Ruiz hummed, clearly impressed.

'Congratulations. It's not everyone who gets the chance to start their working life in London at the top of the tree.'

'It's not that much of a deal,' Holly admitted. 'You've heard of starting at the bottom? Well, this is the rung below that.'

Ruiz laughed and pushed his coffee cup away. 'Tell me more,' he encouraged.

'I've been hired to work as a gofer on the team who write the agony-aunt column. The post is so low-key it's practically invisible. I'm guessing that as long as my coffee-making technique is up to scratch, I'll be fine.'

'Well, at least you're doing your research,' Ruiz pointed out, adopting a mock-serious expression as he glanced at their empty cups.

Holly laughed. 'What about you?' She blushed as Ruiz angled his chin to stare at her. 'I'm sorry. I'm doing it again, aren't I?' she said. 'You must think I'm rude asking you all these questions when we've only just met.'

'No,' Ruiz argued. 'I think you're a cute kid.'

*Ouch.*

'I think you'll make an excellent journalist one day.'

'Is that a polite way of saying nosey's in my genes?'

'No. It means you're interested in the world and those around you,' Ruiz observed.

She wasn't going to argue with him—especially as Holly's world had just shrunk to the size of their table.

'So, Holly-would-be-journalist, just for the record, I do love skiing and riding the waves, so you were right as far as that goes, but bumming around the world is not what I do.'

'What is?'

Touching his nose, Ruiz grinned. 'Look at it this way. Your interview technique can only get better from here on in.'

It would have to, Holly thought wryly, or she'd have nothing to write about. 'Well, thank you for allowing me to try it out on you.'

'Don't mention it,' Ruiz said with amusement, sexy lips pressing down.

And just as Holly was wondering how she could ever bear to look away and bring this folly to an end the waitress handed them the bill.

The café was filling up, the girl explained with an apologetic shrug, and they needed the table.

'It's lunchtime and people are keen to get out of the rain,' Holly agreed, already on her feet. She had taken up enough of Ruiz's time. She made a grab for the bill, but he was too fast for her. 'My treat, remember?' he said. 'And if you change your mind about the dry-cleaning...'

'I won't.' And then finally, as she extended the handle on her suitcase, Holly's phone rang.

'Let me help you,' Ruiz suggested as she attempted to juggle her belongings and the phone.

Checking the number with relief, she answered and said quickly, 'Can you give me a minute?' Then holding the phone to her chest, she put Ruiz off as politely as she could. 'That's okay, honestly. I've got it. Sorry.'

'You're sorry again?' Ruiz murmured dryly, the attractive crease down his cheek reappearing as he smiled. 'You spend a lot of time being sorry, Holly...'

She didn't know what to say to that, and stared at him, hoping she would remember that dark, compelling stare as well as the last delicious punch to her senses that came with it. 'Bye, Ruiz. Thank you for lunch.'

'Goodbye, Holly,' he called after her as she raced outside to take Lucia's call.

Lucia rattled off five numbers. 'Got it?' Lucia demanded.

'Got it,' Holly confirmed, her heart still pounding from the last moments with Ruiz.

'You sound out of breath,' Lucia observed suspiciously. 'I didn't interrupt anything important, did I?'

'Not the sort of *anything* you've got in mind,' Holly protested, laughing. 'The café you recommended was just so noisy I had to run outside to take your call.'

'Just so long as you remember the numbers.'

'I will,' Holly promised, reciting the code Lucia had given her. So the great adventure begins, she thought, staring up at the impressive Palladian mansion across the street.

Nice. Very nice—if a little unsophisticated for his taste, but variety was the spice of life, Ruiz reminded himself as he strode back to his town house with Bouncer in tow. Would he see her again, or would Holly simply disappear into the great melting pot of the metropolis? He liked her a lot. In fact, he couldn't remember a woman making such a strong impression on him in so short a time. Perhaps it was because she made him laugh, or was it that clear green gaze he had found so open and expressive? He could even remember the scent she had used—fresh, citrusy, with just a hint of vanilla. He liked her mouth too—especially when she bit down on the swell of her bottom lip as if that would stop her asking him any more questions. And when she smiled—

'Hey, Bouncer, you liked her, didn't you?'

Soulful eyes turned his way, reminding him he had to find a solution for Bouncer before he returned to Argentina for the polo match…

No. Forget it. That would never work. The idea was ridiculous. He hardly knew Holly and the chances of ever seeing her again were remote. Though he couldn't help wishing he might, Ruiz realised.

Oblivious to the filthy weather, he turned in through the gates of the park. It wasn't the pampas but at least it was a big green space in the middle of the city where the big dog could enjoy some sort of freedom. When Bouncer had first wandered into his life he had intended to turn him over to the police, but when the moment had arrived he hadn't been able to bring himself to do it, and so he'd reported Bouncer missing and taken him home. They'd been together ever since. There had to be some sort of reward for a dog who had sensed an animal lover in a world of pet-free pavements, Ruiz reflected as he reached for the ball he'd stuffed in his pocket. Firing the ball across the park, he had to admit his brother Nacho was right—Ruiz shouldn't have taken the big dog on, only to keep him confined in London.

'Time is running out for us, boy,' he told Bouncer when the dog came bounding back. Ruiz shot the ball again, and felt his heart jag when Bouncer, having joyfully snatched it up, came racing back to him. Was it wrong to hope fate would smile on them? Ruiz reflected as the big dog dropped the ball at his feet. And then he remembered Holly and wondered if it already had.

# CHAPTER TWO

*London Diary:*
*If at first you don't succeed—*
*GIVE UP*

No!
  No. That wasn't what she meant to write at all.
  So. Delete that and start again.
  Okay…

*You'd think it would be seventh heaven living in the Acosta family penthouse with all that space, state-of-the-art gizmos, and furnishings courtesy of a top interior designer, but actually it means not using anything in the kitchen in case you scratch, burn, or break it. And don't get me started on the bathroom. Basically, I'm fed up with tiptoeing around. I might be living in the city, but I'm still a countrygirl at heart. \*Think\* Bigfoot with ten carrier bags on each arm blundering through the glass department at Harrods—and you're still not even close. And then there's the job at ROCK! Working at the hottest magazine in town should be a dream come true, right? Wrong. Things really couldn't get any worse—until you come to my love life.*

*Love life still zero, though lustful thoughts are on
the up, thanks to the man I met at the café called
Ruiz, who looks like a sex god and who thinks I'm
a 'cute kid'.*
*Oh, good. I am a twenty-three-year-old 'kid' with
breasts and a Brazilian.*
*The wax?*
*I always was the glass-half-full type of girl, and
judging by the pressure on the front of Ruiz's jeans
he could fill that glass very nicely indeed.*

Not that she was looking for a boyfriend, but her readers didn't need to know that where Holly was concerned
it was a case of once bitten for ever shy. She had to light
up the page not dwell on her mistakes, because it was all
going wrong at *ROCK!* The job that should have been
perfect for her, where she could be involved in things
that mattered by working on the agony-aunt column, in
however lowly a position, was on the line. She stared at
the latest e-mail memo on her screen; it seemed she was
about to be booted before she even got a chance to prove
what she could do.

Latest figures dire. Agony column doomed unless
reader numbers improve significantly. Need a
diary feature to head the column—something
juicy. Go, team! And remember: last in, first out.
That means you, Holly.

Forcing her chin up, Holly flashed a promise-to-
do-better smile at the staffer who had circulated the
mail. What was Holly supposed to do to make things
better—unless readers would be interested in the in-

credible-disappearing-sock story, or perhaps the find-a-white-bra-amidst-the-various-shades-of-grey scoop?

'I'm on it,' Holly assured the staffer on her way out of the office that night, adopting a seriously concerned expression. She was seriously concerned—for her job.

The staffer managed an even more seriously concerned expression. 'Don't want to lose you, Holly, but…'

The staffer was right. The column was dead unless someone came up with an idea fast.

Hiding behind other people's problems instead of risking another Holly-picks-the-wrong-man-again screw-up had been an attractive proposition when she'd first come down to London, Holly reflected as she walked briskly through the Christmas shopping crowds to the bus stop. But now all she wanted was to take her new life by the scruff of the neck and make a success of it. Her days of hiding behind anything were over. And with no reader letters to answer hiding behind other people's problems wasn't an option, anyway. The sticking point with the failing agony-aunt column was that no one cared any more—people just moved on to the next relationship. It was uncool to admit you needed advice. She had to come up with something novel. If she failed she'd be back at that door with the peeling paintwork and steel mesh security panel to prevent it being kicked in, otherwise known as her first job disaster.

She'd been straight out of college and green as a cabbage when she rocked up at *Frenzy*, a well known magazine. Well-ish known, Holly amended, hailing a bus. She had thought herself really lucky to have such an exciting opportunity straight out of college, in what had turned out to be a badly lit call centre. 'I'm supposed to be on the features desk?' she had explained to the old man in carpet slippers who'd shown her around. It had turned

out Holly's desk was a length of chipped and yellow-
ing plywood facing a peeling wall and she was to share
said desk with around twenty other girls. The girls had
been too busy speaking on the phone to notice Holly's
arrival, and at first she hadn't been able to figure out
why they were all working from dog-eared scripts and
panting into microphones—until her mind had flicked
rapidly through the pages of the magazine. *Frenzy* was
quite raunchy, though nothing out of the ordinary until
you came to the back pages where there were a lot of
ads for services like Personal Tarot Readings, Massage
By Britain's Strongest Woman, or Chat To Chantelle In
Perfect Confidence—

Oh…

'Erm…I'd like to see my supervisor, please.'

And that had been the end of that.

She definitely wasn't going back to some telephone
sex dungeon, Holly determined as she arrived at the penthouse—or Acosta heaven, as she had come to think of
her temporary lodgings. She was going to stay at *ROCK!*
and make a success of the job she had. Once through the
door, she carefully removed her shoes to preserve the
immaculate gleam of the highly polished wooden floor.
Shrugging her coat off, she draped it on a chair, shooting
her bag, briefcase, newspaper, magazines and scarf into
the mix. Just think. If she made a success of her career
as a journalist she could own something like this herself
one day…

Dream on, Holly thought, turning full circle in the
huge marble-tiled hall. A vaulted glass ceiling with a
fabulous view of the stars glittered overhead, while life-
sized Roman busts that might have been originals from
antiquity for all she knew stood on pedestals either side
of the huge double doors. Not only was the cost of a place

like this far beyond Holly's wildest dreams, she would also have to learn how not to be clumsy. A lesson too far, perhaps? No wonder she felt on edge amidst this splendour—one sneeze and she could be bankrupt for life. But for now the penthouse was home, so she might as well make the most of it. Tonight was green face mask night. She did all her best thinking in the bath, so this soak was set to be a long one.

Fate played strange tricks sometimes, Ruiz thought, frowning thoughtfully as he put the phone down and sat back. After he'd been searching high and low for his sister, Lucia had called him up out of the blue, unprompted. He might have known if it was a question of loyalty to a friend, Lucia would break cover immediately. There had been a swift exchange of information and a deal had been brokered between them. Like Nacho, Ruiz was keen for his kid sister to make use of her qualifications rather than to waste her time hanging around the party circuit. Lucia would return to the real world if he agreed to maintain his silence on her current whereabouts. 'But get home fast. On the next flight,' he stressed.

'So you don't mind my friend Holly staying at the penthouse?'

'Not at all.' Fate was definitely playing into his hands, Ruiz reflected while Bouncer murmured with contentment as he rearranged his massive furry body on Ruiz's feet. Apart from the dog's future looking a whole lot rosier, Ruiz had asked enough questions to establish that the Holly he had met at the café and had felt an instant connection with was the same friend his sister had forgotten she had invited to stay. Confirmation of this had elicited several squeals of excitement from Lucia when she realised he had already met her best friend, while he was more than looking forward to a return match with Holly. And as for making up for his sister's oversight—

'There's just one thing, Ruiz,' Lucia said, interrupting these thoughts.

'Which is?' he prompted.

'I gave Holly the impression that she would have the penthouse to herself.'

'How was I supposed to know my town house would flood?'

'Of course you couldn't know, but—'

'I need somewhere to stay,' he pointed out. 'My town house is within walking distance of the penthouse, so it makes perfect sense for me to stay there while the repairs are being carried out. I can keep an eye on the builders that way. Your friend Holly will just have to make room for me.' Lucia knew as well as he that the penthouse had more than enough bedrooms and could comfortably fit a medium-sized house within its walls.

'I'm sure she will,' Lucia insisted. 'I'm just asking you to be diplomatic, Ruiz.'

'Aren't I always?'

'Er, no,' his sister said.

'There's a first time for everything, Lucia.'

'Yeah, right.'

'Is that it?' he asked impatiently.

'Play nice, Ruiz.'

That was easy. 'I promise.'

'Not too nice,' Lucia added, concern returning to her voice. 'Please try to remember that Holly is a good friend of mine.'

'How could I forget?' he said dryly. 'Come on, Bouncer,' he prompted. 'I bet there's a brand-new sofa at the penthouse for you to chomp on.' There was certainly a female interest for Ruiz.

Scenting change in the air, Bouncer lifted his head to look at him. 'You're right,' Ruiz agreed. 'What are we waiting for? Let's get moved in.'

This was the first time she had relaxed properly since arriving in London, Holly realised as she settled back in the deliciously scented foam bath. It was the first time she had trialled a bright green face pack also. Attempting to move her mouth, she quickly forgot the idea in case the face pack cracked. She also had a gloopy oil treatment on her hair and cooling discs of cucumber balanced precariously on her face to soothe her resting eyes. All these preparations were essential for clearing her mind ready for the Great Idea to drop in. It was a little worrying that so far no idea, great or otherwise, had shown the slightest inclination to drop by—

*What was that?*

Shooting up in alarm when she heard the front door opening, she snatched the cucumber from her eyes, switched off the bubbles and remained still, listening.

When she recognised the voice of the intruder she cracked the face pack.

What the hell was *he* doing here?

And should she be in any doubt at all as to the identity of the intruder a big dog was barking excitedly.

He hammered on the bathroom door. What the hell was Holly doing? He had arrived at the penthouse with all sorts of images in his mind—Holly freshly showered and scented, with her hair clean and gleaming, falling in soft waves around her shoulders, Holly with rosy cheeks instead of frozen-to-the marrow cheeks, her green eyes in harmony with the big smile on her welcoming face. He had not expected to discover that Holly appeared to be holding a garage sale in the hall—or to trip over the handles of her briefcase. Having expended some of his irritation in a few, well-chosen words, he now discovered she was in the bath.

This wasn't going to plan. What was he supposed to do now?

'Open this door now,' he commanded.

What should she do? Holly wondered, still cowering in the bath. Ruiz from the café was threatening to break the door down. This didn't make any sense. Who was he? Some kind of crazy? Had he followed her? More importantly, was he dangerous? 'Where did you get the key?' she yelled out.

'From the key box,' he yelled back.

'And the code?' she said suspiciously.

'From my sister.'

'Your sister?' Holly's brain went into overdrive, and then crashed.

'My sister, Lucia Acosta,' Ruiz shouted through the door.

Yes, she'd got that far.

So Ruiz was one of the notorious Acosta brothers. Holly had never met Lucia's playboy brothers so couldn't claim to know much about them, but she did know they were polo-playing bad boys, who, according to Lucia, rode rampage through the world's women as well as their opponents on the field of play. 'And what are you doing here?' she demanded, swishing bubbles over her naked bits.

'More questions, Holly?'

He could laugh at a time like this?

'Why don't you come out of the bathroom and speak to me face to face?' Ruiz challenged.

Yes, she would, Holly determined, firming her jaw.

She wasn't going to cower in the bath. The house might belong to the Acosta family, but Lucia had been very clear when she had told Holly that the penthouse was empty and that Holly could have exclusive use of it until she found somewhere else to live. Lucia hadn't mentioned brothers barging in without warning. 'Shouldn't you be in Argentina playing polo?' she countered, playing for time as she turned the shower on to rinse the gunk out of her hair

'I live and work in London,' Ruiz called back. 'Will you be long?'

'As long as it takes.' Did her nipples have to respond with such a ridiculous amount of interest to Ruiz's shiver-inducing drawl?

Snagging a robe from the hook on the back of the door, she prepared to confront him. Belting it tightly, she reminded herself that new Holly didn't run away, and that new Holly stayed to fight her corner. Braced for battle, she swung the door wide. They stood confronting each other for a moment and then Ruiz began to laugh. 'What?' Holly demanded. It was only when her frown deepened and bits of green gunk started dropping onto the floor that she realised she had forgotten to rinse the face mask off. With an imperious tilt to her chin, she backed into the bathroom and closed the door.

'Would you like me to come back later?' Ruiz jibed through the door.

Holly responded with something unrepeatable that only made him laugh. She quickly washed the face mask off with ice-cold water. She needed a shock to get over seeing Ruiz again. He shouldn't be so stunning. It wasn't fair.

'Perhaps you'd like more time to compose yourself?' Ruiz growled through the door.

'I'm ready to see you any day of the week,' she assured him, flinging it open. Okay, but maybe not today, Holly conceded as Ruiz gave her a lazy twice-over.

'Something bothering you?' he enquired.

'I'm perfectly calm,' she said as her cheeks fired red.

Ruiz met this with a sceptical huff. 'Even when I tell you I'm planning to move in?'

'You can't move in!' Holly exclaimed.

'Can't?' Ruiz queried laconically.

'Of course not. I'm living here,' Holly protested indignantly.

'So...?' Ruiz shrugged.

'So Lucia said I could have sole use of the penthouse until I find somewhere else to live, and—'

'And do you have a contract to this effect?' He was beginning to feel more like the big, bad wolf than the brother of Holly's best friend. He was used to sophisticated women who knew the score, rather than girls like Holly, and was torn between indulging her and kissing the breath out of her lungs. Only Lucia's plea that he should be on his best behaviour stood between them.

'No, of course I don't have a contract,' she was protesting. 'How can I when Lucia's in—when Lucia's away,' she amended, clearly uncertain as to how much he knew about his sister's whereabouts. 'We have a verbal agreement.'

'My sister acts on impulse sometimes,' Ruiz agreed, easing confidently onto one hip.

He admired Holly's loyalty and could only imagine how it might be having Lucia as a friend. This felt like new territory to Ruiz. His strategy had already gone out of the window. Then he was distracted by something flimsy and pink on the floor and noticed Holly's face had turned a deeper shade of pink when she saw him looking at it. She quickly toed away the racy thong. 'Lucia must have warned you I was coming?' he pressed. 'I can't imagine my sister didn't call you.'

'Probably a thousand times,' Holly agreed, no doubt imagining her best friend's panic. 'But my phone is in the bedroom.'

She saw the tension in Ruiz's shoulders relax a little, but as he slowly looked her up and down Holly was sure that lazy gaze could easily penetrate anything as mundane as towelling.

'Well, I'm here now. So I advise you to get used to it, Holly. May I suggest you get dressed while I go and settle Bouncer in?'

'Bouncer?' Holly exclaimed. She couldn't hide the panic in her voice. 'Is it wise to bring Bouncer in here?' The damage the big dog could do to all the treasures in the penthouse didn't bear thinking about.

'Would you prefer me to leave him on the street?'

'No, of course not, but—'

'Or put him into kennels while my town house is being repaired?'

'That would only distress him. You told me he's a rescue dog.'

'Precisely,' Ruiz interrupted. He was serious for a moment, and then his expression changed to one Holly didn't like at all. 'I imagine Bouncer could have a field day in here unless he was properly supervised…'

'I agree,' she said. She didn't like Ruiz's tone, but it did seem as if he might have seen the light where the dangers of breakages were concerned.

'But with you to watch him while I'm away—'

'Me?' Holly exclaimed. 'You can't go away and leave Bouncer with me.'

Recognising his name, Bouncer, no doubt remembering the fuss Holly had given him the first time they met, padded over to the bathroom door and sat at her feet. What was she supposed to do? Ignore him? Bending down, she gave the dog a proper welcome, which Bouncer took as his cue to clean her all over again.

'Look how pleased he is to see you,' Ruiz said in a coaxing tone that set more alarm bells than ever ringing. 'How can you possibly turn him away?'

Holly sighed, but the look she reserved for Ruiz was not at all kind-hearted. He got the special hard look she was working on to deter those who thought they could put one over on new Holly. Ruiz responded to this with the lift of one ebony brow and a look that reminded Holly that, unlike his dog, Ruiz was dangerous. The Acosta brothers were notorious playboys with hair-raising reputations, and like Lucia, they inhabited a very different world from Holly.

So? Keep your nerve and fight fire with fire.

'Bouncer,' Holly murmured fondly, choosing to ignore the dog's master for now. 'Are you looking for a little mayhem?' Gazing up, she threw the gauntlet straight back in Ruiz's face. 'You are? Good boy. There's a lot of scope for you here.' Game on.

The look Ruiz gave her now made Holly's heart beat a rapid tattoo. She should have remembered that Ruiz Acosta was an international sportsman who liked nothing better than a challenge, and in spite of her tough talk Holly's self-confidence was as fragile as a sugar strand. Making her handsome parents proud of their unaccountably plain daughter by winning a full scholarship to a prestigious school had been one of the high spots of Holly's life, until she'd discovered how the other, more privileged girls had felt about it. It was only when Lucia, easily the most envied girl in the school, had palled up with her that Holly's confidence had slowly returned. Well, that sugar strand had just snapped and now she was steeped in self-doubt again.

'I'm going to have a beer and then I'm going to the gym,' Ruiz said. 'Make sure you've cleared up your mess by the time I get back.'

Yes, master. Holly's face burned red, but for once she remained sensibly silent.

Please don't hurry back, Holly thought, catching her breath against the bathroom door. She needed time to think. She could hear Ruiz moving about in the kitchen, but for a moment she did nothing, thought nothing, barely breathed, until, pulling herself round, she came to exactly the same conclusion: this wasn't going to work. Living with a playboy when she was still recovering from the most disastrous love affair of all time? How could she share the same space as a man as brazenly masculine and as unswervingly domineering as Ruiz Acosta? If Ruiz was moving in, she was moving out—

And that was exactly what she would have done had not sensible Holly chosen that moment to intervene and remind flustered Holly that she would still have to sort out alternative accommodation first, and that in the meantime she had no alternative other than to get along with Ruiz. Let's face it, she thought our paths don't even need to cross in a penthouse this size.

'Can we just get one thing straight?' she said to Ruiz, entering the kitchen after having thrown on her fat jeans, as opposed to her I've-lost-weight jeans, together with her oldest, most comfortable shirt. She had left her hair to dry naturally, and bother the make-up—she wasn't interested in men. She merely wanted to catch Ruiz before he left for the gym and set a few things straight.

He paused with the bottle of beer hovering close to his mouth.

*Sexy mouth*…

Concentrate, Holly told herself firmly. They had to get things out in the open if living together stood any chance of working.

'Yes?' Ruiz prompted.

Did he have to have such gorgeous eyes? Did he have to angle that stubble-shaded chin to stare at her? Did his mouth have to curve in that infectious and very dangerous smile? 'When you say you're going away,' she said, feeling her throat dry as she forced her gaze somewhere to the west of Ruiz's left ear, 'don't you mean going away as in flying to Argentina to play polo with your brothers?'

'That will be my next trip,' Ruiz confirmed, his dark eyes watchful.

'So this isn't just the occasional weekend we're talking about—this is full-on adoption of a huge, lollopy dog.'

'Temporary guardianship,' Ruiz corrected her, 'of my dog.'

He made it sound like a royal command—a privilege. And if there hadn't been such a lovely dog involved…

Ruiz showed no shame, Holly concluded. 'You're going to leave Bouncer at the penthouse I've been cautiously tiptoeing around. May I remind you that Bouncer has a huge fluffy tail and four big feet?'

'Your feet are lovely,' Ruiz observed, completely taking the wind out of her sails.

He wasn't supposed to say things like that and sound as if he meant it. Now all she could think about was the fact that she hadn't put shoes on because she'd been in too much of a hurry to speak to Ruiz before he went out.

Concentrate, Holly told herself fiercely as Ruiz

curved a questioning smile. There was no point giving him any more satisfaction than she already had. 'What you're suggesting,' she hissed in a low, urgent voice as if Bouncer could understand them, 'is a licence for carnage.' Couldn't she create enough of that on her own? Holly reasoned. She was just recoiling from the mental image of the type of carnage Bouncer could create when The Idea dropped in.

No one said it was going to arrive at the most convenient time, Holly reasoned as Ruiz began to frown. 'What now?' she prompted.

'I was just thinking that it's not like you to be silent for so long. You are feeling okay, aren't you?' Holly's warning look only succeeded in making Ruiz's eyes glow a little brighter. 'Anyway,' he added offhandedly, 'I'm going out.'

But she wanted to float her idea. 'No, wait.'

'Missing me already?' Ruiz suggested with maximum irony.

'Not one bit,' she snapped. 'In fact, please don't feel you must hurry back.'

This provoked a crooked smile that lodged attractively in Ruiz's stubble-darkened cheek. 'I love it when a plan comes together, don't you?' he said. And when Holly gritted her teeth in order not to say something she would regret, he added, 'I understand you'd probably like a little time to prepare yourself properly for my return.'

'Prepare myself properly?' Holly exploded. 'Who do you think you are? The Sheikh of Araby? I was merely pondering the possibility of doing some work without any further interruption,' she assured him primly.

'Oh, come on, Holly,' Ruiz murmured. 'You and I both know that too much work and no play will make you a very dull girl indeed. See you after the gym?' he said, his eyes dark and dangerous.

'I can't wait,' Holly called after him sarcastically. Living with a playboy wouldn't be easy, but at least Ruiz had given her The Idea.

Bravo! Holly-the-journalist!

Except...there was one small problem. She already knew Ruiz didn't like Holly poking her nose into his business.

But what was he going to do—refuse her offer to dog-sit in London while he was playing polo in Argentina? She didn't think so. She'd seen the glint in Ruiz's eyes. He'd gone in hard, thinking she would quickly fall into line. He had expected her to offer to help him in any way she could. Well, she might—on one condition that Ruiz helped her too. He must give her some titbits to write about. If he did, living with a playboy might not be so bad after all. In fact, it might just save her bacon. The column she had in mind would be an observational piece—meaning she could safely witness the life of a playboy while remaining at a prudent distance. This would be like confronting her demons from behind a screen. To save her career she would lift the lid on living with a playboy for her readers. Why shouldn't everyone else laugh at her trials and tribulations? She did.

Slinging his gym bag over his shoulder, he left his luggage in the hall and stormed out of the penthouse. The only solution, Ruiz had concluded, was to pound his way out of frustration. Having been knocked for six—or was that sex?—by the sight of Holly with her glorious red-gold hair streaming around her shoulders like a gleaming cape, Holly half naked with her creamy flesh just visible above the robe, he was painfully threatening to burst out of his jeans. In that respect, she had exceeded his expectations. Truthfully? He had never felt like this before. If Holly had been staying in Lucia's garden apartment he could have just about coped, but having her stay with him at the penthouse only yards from his bed?

Gritting his teeth, Ruiz lifted his own body weight above his head, but nothing helped to blank out the voluptuous woman waiting for him back at the penthouse. And hard as he tried he could find no solution to the problem. He wouldn't touch a friend of Lucia's. He couldn't eject a friend of Lucia's from the penthouse, either. So must he put his own life on hold? He could hardly entertain while Holly was in residence. Lowering the bar slowly back into its cups, he made a silent pledge not to go near her. He could only hope for Holly's sake that she found somewhere else to live as soon as she could.

He had left Bouncer with the girls on Reception where his faithful hound was sure to get a spoiling. The dog bounded up to him, seeming as excited as he was at the prospect of returning home.

Not excited, Ruiz told himself firmly. Certainly not excited to get back to the penthouse and find Holly waiting for him. It had been a long, hard day, and when he opened the door on what was supposed to be a luxurious hideaway in the best part of London, there would be girl stuff everywhere. No doubt the kitchen would be a mess, and, having seen the state of the hall, he had no doubt Holly would have trialled every bathroom by the time he got back, strewing damp towels all over the place. All he longed for was a good night's sleep, but with a big dog to care for checking into a hotel was out of the question. The penthouse, with its stunning views of London and seductive luxury, should have been perfect, and it might have been, had he not had an unexpected—and frustratingly unsettling—lodger to entertain.

Okay, so he'd set some ground rules.

'Come on, Bouncer,' Ruiz prompted, snapping the leash onto the dog's collar. 'Let's get this over with.'

# CHAPTER THREE

*Research. And that's all it would be. I wouldn't be breaking rule two—no men. I would simply be observing this man from a purely clinical point of view. My 'Living with a Playboy' idea would be like one of those fly-on-the-wall documentaries. I wouldn't be hands-on—I should be so lucky. More, all hands to the pump—gulp—as I try to do my bit to save the agony-aunt column. (Though I can't deny the thought of living so close to this particular playboy has done wonders for my metabolic rate. I've eaten a whole tub of double chocolate chip in anticipation of his return and I can still get into my jeans.)*

*(Imagine how slim I'd be if we lived together permanently.)*

*(Not that I'd ever consider living with anyone after my experience with the ex.)*

*Love life? Vicarious. Active. Very active indeed. Lustful thoughts? Are there any other kind? And the playboy? This might all be over by tomorrow. He didn't exactly seem thrilled to see me, and I have yet to discover how he feels when he returns from the gym to find I'm still here.*

HAVING finished her London diary entry, Holly was still tinkering with her first 'Living with a Playboy' feature when Ruiz arrived back. The new headline looked fabulous on the top of the agony-aunt column. If that didn't attract reader interest, nothing would.

She listened as Ruiz went into one of the bathrooms to take a shower and tried her hardest not to imagine him stripped naked. That proved a lot harder than she'd thought. The secret of successful cohabiting was not getting in Ruiz's way, Holly concluded, tensing as the shower turned off. If she was going to make a success of the 'Living with a Playboy' feature, she had to make sure Ruiz didn't think of her as a nuisance, always watching him and asking questions. She wasn't in any danger, she told herself repeatedly, counting the seconds until he entered the room, since she had vowed off men, and anyway there was no chance Ruiz would look at her that way. The main thing was not to give him an excuse to throw her out if she was going to make him the subject of her column.

Buttering-up time had arrived. While he'd been gone she had tidied away all her things and knocked up a tasty soup, using the fresh ingredients she had bought earlier. She'd also made sure there was plenty of ice for the large gin and tonic she guessed a sophisticated man like Ruiz might want, and had even put on some make-up—not very expertly, and certainly not enough to suggest she was after him. She hoped that assuming the role of unthreatening temporary lodger might work. She would even play housekeeper at a stretch. She'd do anything to salvage her career. She'd even iron a few shirts if she had to. She couldn't see any man objecting to that. Whatever it took for Ruiz to agree to become the subject of her column, Holly told herself tensely, flinging herself down in front of her laptop when she heard him advancing on the kitchen.

> *Living with a Playboy*
> *Well, here I am, living the dream—or nightmare— not sure which it's going to be yet. I should know more if I survive these next few minutes.*
> *I don't think I could have engineered living with a playboy. Who could, unless they wanted to be a rich man's plaything? And I can't say that's ever appealed to me. But I will do my best to keep a roof over my head until I can make alternative arrangements. I don't particularly like myself for being so cold-blooded about this, but it's the only solution I can see to keep my job right now.*
> *To make up for my scheming I'm going to be the best housemate anyone could have—at least, that's what I keep telling myself. But the first time the playboy brings home a playmate I'm guessing I might show another side of myself altogether. It's not that I'm interested in him, and he certainly isn't interested in me. This is all in the line of duty, and—*

Lowering the lid on her laptop, Holly arranged her face in a welcoming smile and stood up to greet Ruiz. Enter Ruiz: dark, glowering, massively powerful, and stunningly attractive. 'Hello,' Holly said brightly. 'I hope you had a good session at the gym?'

As Ruiz angled his head slightly to stare at her Holly realised she would never be able to keep this up. Faced by so much pumped and bulging muscle and with his thick black hair still damp from his shower, she knew she couldn't live with Ruiz as a passive observer without going completely off her head. 'Drink?' she enquired. Was that piping voice really hers? 'Gin and tonic, perhaps…?'

'A beer would be good.'

'Beer it is, then.'

'You're unusually compliant, Holly,' Ruiz observed, narrowing his eyes suspiciously.

She made a dismissive gesture. 'I'm just feeling a little guilty that I didn't make the connection between you and Lucia right away. When we first met at the café?' she prompted.

'I didn't make the connection either,' Ruiz pointed out. 'And Lucia told you what exactly about her brothers?'

Holly blushed. The thought of even the smallest part of what Lucia had told her about her brothers was enough to make the hair stand up on the back of her neck. 'You must be stressed out and tired,' she said to change the subject, 'and frustrated that you haven't got the private space you anticipated, but—'

'Breathe,' Ruiz suggested dryly.

Ruiz's dark gaze washed over her in a way that made her bones melt. She had dressed carefully—demurely— on purpose, Holly realised now, in a pair of baggy jeans and a shapeless old shirt, so as not to draw attention. She suspected Ruiz knew exactly what she'd done, and that he also knew she was suffering a very female response to his extremely masculine assessment.

'Where's that beer you promised me?'

Maybe this subservient domestic goddess role was going to be a little harder than she thought, Holly reflected, realising she was still gazing at Ruiz. 'Coming right up,' she said, forcing her feet to walk away.

Her hands were shaking by the time she got to the fridge and her heart was beating like Thor's hammer.

How on earth was this going to play out? Her bright idea of making a column out of living with a playboy didn't seem so clever now. Being sneaky didn't suit her, and a high-flyer like Ruiz would hardly want Holly sharing details of his private life with the general public. But she had to live somewhere. She had to earn a living. And this was the best, the only idea she had come up with to date.

'Thank you.' His gaze lingered on Holly as he took the beer. He'd run the shower on its lowest setting to try and knock some sense into his head, but innocence was a potent drug. He noticed her hands were shaking and guessed Holly was still reeling from the messy relationship Lucia had told him about and didn't trust her judgment where men were concerned. No problem for him. He could resist the lure of an unexpected visitor, however attractive she might be.

'Are you hungry, Ruiz?'

The punch to his solar plexus when she turned to look at him caught him by surprise. 'Starving.'

'You're in a better mood since you got back from the gym,' she observed as she vigorously stirred the soup.

'Yes, dear,' he mocked her lightly.

'And here was me thinking you might have knocked some of that frustration out of your system at the gym.' She blushed and stopped talking abruptly, but he knew she was referring to his ill-tempered arrival at the penthouse.

Lifting the bottle in a toast to her back, he drank it down. He had dressed casually after his shower in a pair of jeans and an old, faded blue sweatshirt, which he felt comfortable in around the house. Holly was barefoot in jeans and a pale blue shirt, which he found both casual and appealing. She was wearing hardly any make-up and had a tea towel tucked into the waistband of her jeans like

someone who loved cooking and didn't care who knew
it. She looked great. The pale blue shirt suited her, and
he had to try very hard not to notice that it was strain-
ing over her breasts.

'Sure soup is going to be enough for you?' she asked,
avoiding his gaze.

'For now.'

Opening the fridge, he found it stocked with fresh ingredients and a line of cold beer. 'Soup smells good,' he
observed, joining Holly at the cooker. 'I usually call for
take-away when I'm in London, unless I'm eating out—'
He was staring at the back of her neck, longing to drop
kisses on it. She had brushed her hair to one side, leaving the soft skin temptingly exposed, and he was standing close enough to see it had the texture of a peach. 'Are
you sure you want to share your supper?' he murmured,
thinking of anything but soup.

'I can't drink the whole pan full myself.' She turned
to stare at him.

'I'll get some spoons,' he said, breaking away first,
knowing that if he didn't he would have to take her to
bed.

'I'm sorry for our rocky start this evening, Ruiz. I
hope the soup makes up for it.'

'I'm sorry too,' he said. 'I was hardly Señor Charming
earlier.' She was a friend of his sister's, he told himself
sternly. It was his duty to be nice to her. Equally, it was
his duty not to seduce her. 'Why don't we forget it and
start over? Minestrone.' He hummed with appreciation.
'My favourite.'

'Really?' She seemed surprised. 'I had you down as
more of a vichyssoise man.'

'Oh, please. Do you think I have my newspapers
ironed before I read them too?'

'I'll be sure to be up early enough to do so, sir.'

'Be sure you are,' he teased, holding the emerald gaze until her cheeks flushed red.

A friend of his sister's? His good intentions where Holly was concerned weren't holding up too well, Ruiz concluded, registering the pressure in his jeans. 'Hurry up, I'm hungry,' he commanded mock-sternly, hoping that by adopting the role of master of the house he would distract them both.

Holly smiled and shook her head. 'Do you treat all your staff like this?'

'My staff?' he queried.

'The people you pay to do things for you,' she teased him.

'Was that supposed to be a joke?' he countered, finding he couldn't bring himself to avoid the extraordinary green gaze and that he really didn't want to.

'What do you think?' She laughed.

'I think you like living dangerously, Ms Valiant,' he said quietly.

Holly's smile died. He got the distinct impression that this brush with a man who really liked her was too much too soon for Holly. 'Do you think Bouncer would like some soup?' she asked him in a decidedly humourless tone.

'If you sprinkle cheese on it I doubt he could refuse,' he said, matching Holly for matter-of-factness. This was like trying to win the trust of a damaged pony. He couldn't lay his cards on the table—tell her she was beautiful and that he wanted her. He had to earn her trust and wait for Holly to come to him. She was graceful, he thought as she dipped low to feed the dog. She was kind and gentle and funny too. This was proving to be an unexpected distraction and he was enjoying tonight more than he could possibly have imagined.

'I realise this must be awkward for you,' she began as she straightened up.

'Awkward?' he queried.

'Living together like this,' she explained. 'I'm not exactly experienced when it comes to flatmates.'

He doubted she was experienced in any sense. 'Don't worry. You won't be seeing a lot of me.'

She laughed. 'Can I have that in writing, please?'

'And when I'm here I promise to keep out of your way,' he added.

'That's all I need to know,' she said, but her darkening eyes told a different story.

As they settled down to drink the soup together either side of the kitchen table it occurred to him that, as Lucia's friend, Holly was practically an honorary member of the family and so deserving of his protection, which was ironic when what she needed was protection from him.

'Soup okay, Ruiz?'

'It's delicious,' he said. It was. And when she smiled like that, looking so relieved and happy, he knew that Holly was as oblivious to her talents as she was to her beauty. It was when she cut a fresh slice from the crispy loaf, saying, 'I like a man with a healthy appetite,' that he had to reach for the butter and pretend he hadn't heard what she'd said. 'Hey, Bouncer.' He called the dog to draw the spotlight off her. 'Are you snoring?' he suggested as the big mutt grunted in his sleep.

'You're asking questions of a sleeping dog?' Holly enquired, watching him chin on hand.

'Is that permitted?' he teased, thinking how beautiful her eyes were.

Shaking her head, she smiled. 'I think you love that

dog. Don't worry, I'll clear up,' she said, pushing her chair back.

'Let me help you,' he offered, realising how much he wanted to be close to her.

One step at a time, Holly thought, feeling heat curl low inside her when Ruiz brushed past her at the sink. Now, if she could just control that heat and direct it into building a friendship with Ruiz everything might work out fine.

'Why don't you tell me something about the gap between school with my sister and now?' Ruiz suggested casually, taking her off guard as they loaded the dishwasher together. 'You can leave out anything you don't want to talk about.'

'That would mean leaving out most of it,' she said, trying to make a joke of things she really didn't want to remember. 'And I'd much rather talk about you.'

'I'm sure you would,' Ruiz agreed dryly, easing onto one hip.

'A playboy makes a much more interesting topic of conversation than the life of a would-be journalist,' Holly pointed out.

'A playboy?' Ruiz queried. 'Is that how you see me?'

'That's how the world sees you.'

'Really?' His lips pressed down. 'It seems a rather old-fashioned term for a man who works hard for a living.'

'A man who lives like this,' Holly interrupted him, glancing round the designer kitchen. 'Most people would find it fascinating.'

'That's only because they don't know the truth about the boring slog associated with getting to this point,' Ruiz assured her with amusement.

'And if they did?' she said carefully.

'What are you getting at, Holly?'

'Can I be honest with you?'

'I hope you're always honest.'

She braced herself. 'The column I'm working on is failing. If it has any chance of surviving it needs something different, something unique, to draw people in.'

He looked at her for a moment, and then he said, 'Oh, no.'

'Please let me finish,' she begged him. 'I'm proposing to write a fictional piece to head up the column and build reader numbers. I've always kept a personal diary,' Holly explained, 'and this would be a public extension of that—half serious, mostly poking fun at me, ordinary Holly Valiant, living with a glamorous playboy.'

'No,' Ruiz said flatly.

'It was just an idea—'

'You're not ordinary and I'm not glamorous.'

But Ruiz seemed glamorous to her with his wild, thick black hair and swarthy complexion. He was darkly dangerous and dangerously sexy. And readers would love him. He was standing very close—close enough to touch—close enough for her senses to pick up on his mood. It wasn't anger she sensed, but something a lot more worrying.

'And I'm certainly not a playboy,' he added, moving away.

'But who's to know that?' she pressed.

'I can see I'll have to watch what I say to you in future, Holly Valiant.'

So it wasn't a complete no, Holly thought, feeling excitement build inside her. 'I would never write anything derogatory about you.'

'I should think not...' And why was he even giving her this much of an opening? It might amuse him to read it, Ruiz reasoned. 'So is all this talk about a new column just a ruse to get out of telling me about your past?'

'If I tell you about my past you'll be asleep in five minutes,' Holly assured him. 'Why don't you start the ball rolling?' she suggested. 'Just make sure you leave out anything you don't want to see in print,' she added, tongue in cheek.

He stared at her for a moment, and then he laughed. 'Touché, Ms Valiant.'

'*En garde*, Señor Acosta.'

She made him laugh. She made him relax. She made him realise he could enjoy being with a woman without taking her to bed. Who knew? Ruiz mused wryly.

An hour into their chat and they were still going strong. It turned out she did have a talent for teasing out interesting facts, after all. Ruiz had relaxed enough to laugh when she told him about some of her more colourful teenage years. 'There was the home perm, the fake tan incident, and the gothic fright phase that almost got me thrown out of school. I tried to dye my red hair black, and it turned out green.'

When Ruiz pulled a face his sexy mouth pressed down in the most attractive way. 'So what did you get up to?' she pressed.

'Do you mean, what can I tell you about?' Ruiz shook his head as he accepted the challenge. 'I ran away to the pampas when I was about fifteen. When you live on an *estancia* the size of a small country there is only the pampas to run away to.'

'Lucky you.'

'I didn't think so, aged fifteen.'

It was just another form of isolation, Holly mused, thinking back to her own uncertain teenage years.

'I lived like a wild boy off the land.'

And she could picture him with limbs as brown as the parched earth he rode across, and his frame as lean as the predators that circled his campfire each night. 'Weren't you afraid?'

'I was too young to know fear. I was fit and strong, and thought myself invincible.'

She couldn't breathe for a moment, and then the dark eyes that had been dancing with laughter one moment stilled as Ruiz levelled a brooding stare on her face. Lifting one lock of her hair, he curled it around his finger. 'I can't believe you tried to dye your beautiful hair, or that you risked turning it into a frizz with a perm.'

'Risked?' Holly queried, pulling back, wishing she were ready for this and accepting she might never be. 'My hair not only frizzed, it fell out. I thought it would never grow back.'

'You thought no man would ever look at you again?' he suggested.

'It isn't easy being a teenager—for anyone. So, what were you like?' she pressed. 'I mean when you grew out of the running-away-to-the-pampas stage?'

'In my early twenties I was insufferably arrogant.'

'No?' Holly mocked. 'I find that impossible to believe.'

He laughed. 'Believe,' he assured her. 'I was quite ridiculous. And rude.'

'But you're so polite now.'

'Why, thank you. I guess my manners managed somehow to survive those years. I have my older brother Nacho to thank for them. He was always very strict with us.'

'Tell me about him,' Holly pressed. 'Tell me about the band of brothers and your sister Lucia.'

'You probably know Lucia better than I do.' But he

told her how they all felt they owed everything they were and everything they had to Nacho, who had stayed to raise his siblings when their parents had died in a flood.

How could she not warm to this man? Holly wondered as Ruiz's massive shoulders eased in a regretful shrug while he tried and failed to recover memories of his parents from his early childhood. The more she learned about him, the harder it was going to be to live with him and keep things light—let alone write about him with any form of impartiality. Tugging her feet free from Bouncer's furry weight, she left the table for the relative security of the sink. 'I'll finish clearing up,' she offered. 'You can go and—'

'I can go and…what?' Ruiz murmured.

He was standing right behind her, Holly realised, quivering as she felt the caress of Ruiz's breath on her neck. She started to launch into some excuse to move away, but Ruiz was way ahead of her. 'Goodnight, Holly,' he said. 'And thanks for supper. It was great.'

# CHAPTER FOUR

*Reality bites.*
*Love life.*
*Lustful thoughts.*

THE headings for her personal diary were as far as she got. She would have to change her way of working, Holly decided. She didn't want to think too closely about reality where her love life was concerned when the only love life she wanted was one she didn't have the courage to embrace and couldn't have anyway. She would confine her writing to her fictionalised column in *ROCK!* It didn't hurt so much. She couldn't bring herself to be flip or even name the deeper feelings Ruiz had stirred inside her.

'There's no hope for you, Holly Valiant,' she told her reflection in the bedroom mirror. 'You are a lost cause where men are concerned.' But with fair weather and a following wind she might still become a reasonable journalist one day. Opening the lid on her laptop, she began to write.

*The playboy has just moved in, so now we are sharing the same living space courtesy of a humungous screw-up on the part of his sister, my best*

*friend. It's a fabulous penthouse overlooking the
River Thames, the Houses of Parliament, and every
other iconic London building you can think of—I
can see them all from my bedroom window as I
write to you. One day in and I can already tell you
that playboys are just like the rest of us...but I know
that's not what you want to hear. You want to hear
about the fabulous lifestyle, the sex, the drama, and
all the extravagance—for that's how the playboy life
appears to us mere mortals. Whereas owning several homes, a couple of private jets, and having the
tailor come to call on you is commonplace for the
playboy. The only thing I can't tell you about yet is
the sex—it's too soon—but I have no doubt there
will be women flocking round in no time. And I can't
tell you about the tailor, because I made that bit up.
But the playboy...that's another matter. He's no fig-
ment of my imagination. He's hard and tanned, and
stands over six feet tall, with massive shoulders and
impossibly strong forearms. His hair is thick, black
and wild, like a man who answers to no one, and
his eyes are dark and brooding. I've never seen his
face without a coating of sharp black stubble and
his teeth are perfect. You'll have to imagine my sigh
of despondency here, for I am barely five foot three
and I'm a redhead. The type you used to call gin-
gers with a hard 'g' at school? Plus, I always know
the answer to 'Does my bum look big in this?' If this
rings a bell for you, join me, why don't you, on my
journey of discovery? And I'll share everything I
discover about him here with you.*

She could only try, Holly thought, pressing Send. If
the team didn't like the piece they didn't have to run it.

And she couldn't fight the compulsion to write—or, more truthfully, to write about Ruiz. It was probably going to be the only way she could express her feelings for him.

Since their chat she was seeing Ruiz in a completely new light, as a real man, rather than a fantasy figure. Hearing him go into his own room and close the door, she had crept back into the living room with her laptop. A change of scene usually made ideas flow, but it was hard to imagine she would write any more tonight when her head was stubbornly full of strong arms, and strong tanned hands with lean, elegant fingers. No wonder Ruiz was a world-class polo player. She could so easily imagine those powerful thighs wrapped around the sides of a horse, or those sensitive hands lightly fingering the reins.

How was she supposed to sleep when her head was full of that? Thank goodness she was a realist and could channel all her X-rated thoughts into the column. As far as real life was concerned she had done nothing risky other than sit down and have supper with Ruiz, Holly reassured herself, and where was the harm in that?

'What do you think, Bouncer?' she murmured, turning from the makeshift desk she'd created on a table to fluff the animal's massive ears. 'At least you've got the good sense to maintain a neutral silence,' she observed wryly as Bouncer adjusted his position on her feet with a contented sigh. 'I can't think of a better companion to keep me company through the night than you,' she told the big dog fondly.

Which was a pity, Ruiz reflected wryly, standing outside the door. Holly was too innocent and too bruised for someone like him to lead astray. Holly believed in love and happy ever after while his hunting instinct was firmly tuned to the here and now. So what now? Was he supposed to go to bed, close his eyes, forget Holly and drift away? Even his dog had changed allegiances.

He should be pleased about that, Ruiz reminded himself, shooting one last glance through the door at the homely tableau Holly had unwittingly created with Bouncer. If someone was going to take care of the dog while he was away, who better than Holly?

Holly almost fell off her chair when a hand touched her shoulder. 'Ruiz!' Who else could unfurl a starburst of sensation like that? Holly reasoned, swinging round. 'Did I wake you?' she said with concern. 'I'm sorry.'

'I saw the light on,' Ruiz explained.

He was wearing a robe that had fallen open at the front to reveal a torso that would defy her best attempts to describe it to her readers. 'Ripped, tanned, and shaded with just the right amount of dark hair,' would fail utterly to do justice to a body that was unique in Holly's experience. But then she glimpsed the black boxers beneath the loosely fastened belt and knew it was time to look away. 'I should have remembered to shut the door when I put the light on,' she said, blushing furiously.

'It's good you're keen about the job,' Ruiz observed, propping one hip against the end of the table where she was working, 'but don't you think you should get some sleep?'

'I work best at night—and I'm going to bed soon,' she added in response to his sceptical look.

'I suppose I should thank you,' he said.

Ignoring the danger signal that streaked down her spine, she asked him what he meant.

'I couldn't sleep either. I thought I might come in here and watch a game on TV. But if you're working...'

'You can watch TV. It won't disturb me.' And company would be nice, Holly thought, though in Ruiz's case she had yet to discover if she could concentrate while he was in the room.

'No, I think bed is better than dozing on the sofa,' he said, turning for the door. Stretching out a hand, he added casually, 'Are you coming?'

It was a moment before she realised he wasn't talking to Bouncer, but to her. 'Certainly not,' she exclaimed indignantly.

'I was only suggesting you should get some sleep— in your own bed,' Ruiz stressed, to Holly's hot, burning shame.

'In a minute,' she said, bending low over the laptop so that her hair concealed her face. 'I've got a couple of things I need to finish off here first.'

'Would you like me to read what you've written so far?'

'No, thank you.' All her yearning and insecurities written to amuse the reader were a little too close for comfort where Ruiz was concerned. She looked up to him standing over her, his eyes dancing with laughter. 'Have you been reading over my shoulder?'

'Me?' he drawled.

'Yes. You.' Closing the lid on her laptop, she stood to confront him, which involved some serious neck-craning. 'I prefer to finesse my work before I show it to anyone. I'd only be sharing bullet points with you at this juncture.'

'Oh, would you?' he asked, mocking her suddenly starchy English accent with a chocolaty South American drawl. 'Well, if you're quite sure?' The wicked mouth tugged in a sexy grin. 'My sister tells me I'm a very good listener...'

'I'm sure you are,' Holly agreed, then deflated instantly as Ruiz turned for the door. Why had she driven him away? What was wrong with her? 'Do you mind if I keep Bouncer with me tonight?' she said, hardly realising it was an attempt to keep him a moment longer.

'Be my guest,' he said with an expression in his dark, laughing eyes that said as far as attempts to stop him leaving her went, this was lame. 'I'm relieved you and Bouncer get along so well.'

Why were alarm bells ringing? She should have picked Ruiz up on that last remark, Holly realised. She hadn't agreed to dog-sit Bouncer for him, had she? She had a horrible suspicion that Ruiz had taken her agreement to do this for granted.

She handled relationships with animals better than she did with men, Holly reflected, kneeling down so she could cuddle up to some non-judgmental warmth. 'Oh, Bouncer, why am I such a clutz when it comes to men?' She sagged as the door clicked quietly shut.

There was better news for Holly the next morning. The team had not only accepted her first submission to the column, but was delighted and relieved she could deliver a follow-up so quickly. Holly couldn't help but smile when they showed her the first article in print, with her second article already up on the web site. Early signs suggested that hits on the web site had increased, and they had all gathered round to read what she had to say.

*One failed relationship does not a lifetime of disastrous love affairs make. Don't let it rule your life. Don't let it dictate what you should expect from life, or restrict what you achieve, says the redhead who doesn't even register on the playboy's radar—but who would like to. As you may have suspected, liv-*

*ing with a playboy isn't as straightforward, or as glamorous as it sounds. The playboy may see me as a quirky nuisance, but I have all the same lusts and longings as the most beautiful playgirls we've ever featured in ROCK! My trouble is, I waste far too much time wondering how can a girl like me attract a man like that? When the simple answer is: I can't. And why would I want to, when you and I both know I'm looking for something more than a one-night stand—however memorable that one night stand might be. And it would be memorable. But please don't think I'm defeated, because after last night's surprisingly cosy supper chat back at the penthouse I think the playboy and me might have something going on in the friendship department. And friends are one of the most precious things in life, don't you agree?*

There had been friendship between herself and Ruiz last night, hadn't there? Holly fretted as the team congratulated her. She couldn't help but keep running over everything Ruiz and she had said to each other, and had to drag herself back to the present so as not to offend her colleagues when they suggested a celebratory lunch at the local coffee bar.

After lunch, she worked until the end of the day on reader problems. Quite a few more had come in by e-mail. All the team had their heads down, and someone suggested readers might have grown in confidence knowing they wouldn't receive a flip response from someone who was having her own battle with insecurity.

'Let's hope this isn't a flash in the pan,' Holly told the staffer on her way home that evening, when even he had said well done. She could hardly believe it when the king of the sceptics cracked a smile and winked back at her.

Ruiz had arranged a supper date with a woman who always made him laugh. He sat through it glancing at his watch, wondering what Holly was doing at the penthouse. She didn't have many friends in London yet, and with the trouble she'd mentioned at work—the predicted early demise of the agony-aunt column—he guessed she must be feeling low. He made some polite mumble in response to the woman sitting opposite him at the high-end restaurant, but they both knew his thoughts were elsewhere.

'Excuse me, Ruiz.'

He refocused as the woman across the supper table from him touched his hand. 'Forgive me,' he responded. 'It's been one of those days.'

'I can see that,' his blonde companion murmured in a suggestive purr.

'Do you mind if we cut this short?' Even the tone of her voice set his teeth on edge, and they both knew the answer to his question. Players in the field could read each other like well-thumbed books and he was tired of playing the field, or whatever this type of civilised prelude to sex was called. 'Please accept my apologies,' he said, abruptly standing. 'I realise I've been lousy company tonight.'

His companion didn't argue.

Two weeks had passed since her first article for the column, and these days she was rising before dawn to start work on her ideas. There didn't seem to be enough hours in the day now her 'Living with a Playboy' feature had been officially declared a success, but at least that made it easier to live with Ruiz. Keeping busy gave Holly less time to regret that she wasn't a five foot six blonde with more up front than behind, and meant she could channel her energies into the column. Since that night when Ruiz had come back and looked at Holly long and hard as if he were trying to work out what particular brand of sugar and spice she was made of, he had kept away. There had been no more cosy chats. And, of course, that suited her.

No, it didn't. She had spent most of last night wondering where he had spent the night. Plus, her thoughts on Ruiz's lady friends were not all worthy of the girl she used to be. She had become an evil shrew and felt an uncontrollable urge to share this with her readers, who were growing in number by the day. It turned out that even so-called nice girls could discover a very different side to their natures when there was a gorgeous man involved…

Glancing at the stack of newspapers piled neatly by the side of the desk she had improvised in the penthouse, Holly knew she must put Ruiz out of her mind for ten seconds, finish her work, and then study the Classified ad section and circle some rooms to let. She couldn't go on like this. She had to find somewhere to live where she could stand on her own two feet. Frowning as she bent her head over the keyboard again, she completed the advice section for the agony-aunt column and then turned to her next piece for 'Living with a Playboy'.

*I would have stayed in the background as I had intended had it not been for a very expensive pair of designer shoes…*
*Don't believe anyone who tells you women are on the same side when there are shoes and a playboy at stake. In this situation it's a case of survival of*

*the fittest—and I have discovered that I need to
have a serious rethink if I'm going to survive.
Honestly, I don't have a clue. How was I supposed
to know that the high-heeled shoes I found dumped
in the hallway when I got home from work would
lead to a pair of sexy hold-ups artfully draped
over the handle of the living room door? Or that
the woman reclining on the sofa in a bright pink
Basque and a rather scary translucent thong was
expecting our mutual friend to walk in rather than
me?*

*How was I supposed to know she had a key?
I don't know who was more surprised—me, or the
blonde. Anyway, I apologised, and, on my way out
of the room, managed to tumble over her shoes and
snap the heel off. Needless to say, all hell broke
loose. Quickly realising that neither my vocabu-
lary nor my stumpy, bitten nails were up to a cat
fight I took myself off to the bathroom and locked
the door, where I proceeded to sing tunelessly with
my hands over my ears until I heard our mutual
friend arrive. When I removed my hands from my
ears it was to hear him promise to do something
about the mad woman in the flat and replace the
shoes she had destroyed. Traitor, I thought.*

*But the promise of shoes made me think that here
was a man I might be able to do business with...
until I considered this more deeply and realised
that a playboy would never do it for me, because I
want to buy my own shoes and I'm pretty sure one
pair wouldn't be enough...*

Closing the computer, Holly sat back before turning to
her next task. Lifting the newspapers onto the table, she

sorted and stacked them, and then started methodically trawling through the ads. She had a reassuring number of opportunities circled when she heard the front door open and a familiar stride coming her way. Her heart began to thump. It was very early in the day to have any sort of confrontation, let alone be thrown out on the street with some bimbo cheering Ruiz on. It was with enormous relief that she realised he was alone. Opening her laptop again, she pretended to be working when he came into the room.

'Good morning, Holly.'

'Morning,' she said offhandedly. But she rather spoiled the effect by looking up to find Ruiz dressed immaculately in a sharp dark suit, with a crisp white shirt, and a pearl-grey tie. He looked amazing.

'I just got in from Paris,' he explained, dumping an exquisitely wrapped box of tiny rainbow-tinted macaroons on the table in front of her.

'What have I done to deserve this honour?' she enquired in the same cool tone, while hectic images of hysterical girlfriends re-enacting the 'off with her head' scene between the Red Queen and Alice leapt unbidden into her head. Did the Red Queen wear a translucent pink thong, perchance? 'What?' she said as Ruiz shrugged off his jacket, loosened his tie, freed a couple of buttons at the neck of his shirt, and stretched out on the sofa swinging a distinctive carrier bag from a well-known Parisian boutique above his head.

'What size feet have you got?' he asked.

'Isn't that a rather personal question?' There were some things a lady never divulged. Though, to be fair, the shoes she had trashed belonging to Miss Pink Basque had been the same size Holly wore.

'Well, if you don't want them.'

'If I knew what you were talking about…'

'Why don't you come over here and find out?' Ruiz suggested. 'If the shoes are the wrong size you can always take them back to the store and change them.'

'In Paris?'

'No need to sound so snippy,' he said, sitting up to bait her with a stare. 'Not jealous, are we?' And just like that the dark, dangerous eyes were laughing again.

But after the bimbo affair Holly refused to be won over quite so easily. 'I'm not at all jealous of you,' she said crisply. 'I've seen your friends.'

'You've seen a passing acquaintance,' Ruiz assured her, 'who has now passed.'

'Away? How unfortunate.'

'Into history, I was about to say. Don't be sarcastic, Holly,' Ruiz warned, pretending to be stern. 'It doesn't suit you.'

She turned back to the keyboard, hurting inside. Even a mistress who had passed into history was a mistress too far. 'I suppose I can use the story for the column,' she muttered.

'If you don't want the shoes…'

Holly stiffened. 'Are you saying you bought the shoes for me?'

'I bought the blonde shoes—'

'What a gentleman you are,' Holly interrupted acidly. 'How thoughtful of you.'

'Holly,' Ruiz droned good-humouredly, 'I bought the shoes to replace the ones you broke, but the blonde decided she'd prefer a cheque for a somewhat larger amount, so I took the shoes back to the store—'

'Do I need to hear this?'

'I just want to make it clear that I'm not giving you

anyone's leftovers. I bought them for you. Don't you want to see them?'

'For me?' she said suspiciously, hating the way her voice was trembling. 'You bought shoes…for me?' She turned to find Ruiz looking less confident than usual, or maybe she was delusional, which was entirely possible. In the end curiosity got the better of her. There was nothing wrong with taking a look. She could only hope Ruiz's taste in shoes was an improvement on his taste in women. She could fake it for the column, but she was pretty sure she couldn't fake anything for Ruiz, though he stood a serious risk of having the shoes land heavily on his head if this was another of his jokes!

'Before we came to the mutual decision that cash was king the blonde chose some trashy, sparkly things, like the ones you stomped on,' Ruiz explained, handing the box over. 'I thought they looked better in pieces, frankly, and so I chose these. What do you think?'

Did shoe heaven cover it? The leather was the softest she had ever felt, the heel was the highest, the colour was a beautiful pale dove grey. And the sole was scarlet. 'I think…' They're divine, Holly thought, feeling a quiver of excitement at the prospect of wearing them. She could never have afforded shoes like these… 'I think you should return them to the shop,' she said, remembering the advice she had given one of her readers in capital letters on this very subject: 'Never Accept Expensive Gifts From Men. Why? Because it puts you in their debt.' And the piece hadn't even gone to press yet, sensible Holly reminded drooling Holly sternly. 'As they haven't been worn I think you could get a full refund,' she said, placing the shoe back in its box.

'What's wrong with them?' Ruiz demanded, removing his crossed feet from the table and sitting up straight.

'I never accept gifts like this from men.'

'Well, that's a habit you should change right away,' Ruiz observed dryly. 'I suppose it also means I can't take you out to supper tonight—though if you feel badly about it, I can always let you pay…'

Ruiz was asking her out?

No. Ruiz was asking her to take him out, which gave Holly a problem. If this had been a straightforward invitation to supper she could refuse, but seeing as she was taking up half a penthouse that was rightfully his, the least she could do was stand Ruiz a meal…

'Perhaps if we go out I'll get a chance to talk to you about paying a fair rent to live here,' Holly murmured thoughtfully. To date, both Ruiz and Lucia had refused to take any money from her, while Holly's house-hunting efforts had swung disastrously between scratching sounds behind the skirting boards to smelly drains, and even, on one memorable viewing, an infestation of ants. 'Rent?' she prompted, seeing now that there was something very worrying in Ruiz's eyes.

'What a great idea,' he agreed mildly. 'Trust you to come up with something.'

The day improved when Holly arrived at *ROCK!* to find she had been given her own office with two assistants to help her, which she had to take as a sign that the agony-aunt column was on the up. 'But let's not get carried away,' she cautioned the two girls sent to help her. 'This is still early days, and—'

'You've worked a miracle so we can all keep our jobs?' Pixie suggested.

'I wouldn't put it quite like that,' Holly argued red-faced.

'You have to carry on living with the playboy now…

poor you,' Freya said, exchanging a wry look with Pixie. 'Not that we're jealous, or anything.'

What would Ruiz have to say about that? Holly wondered, feeling the buzz inside her ramp up a gear at the thought that she had to go out to supper tonight with him.

'Anyway, we're just glad to be here,' Freya added warmly as she plonked a thriving pot plant, her personalised mug, a budget-sized box of tissues and a generous supply of chocolate for them all to share on the desk.

'You're right,' Holly agreed, telling herself not to be so selfish and join in the celebration. She had to stop wishing and longing, and pretending she could steer her life to a happy-ever-after-ending in which a confident Holly Valiant won the hand of a prince instead of a frog. She could do what she liked through the column, but not that. The 'Living with a Playboy' feature was a fiction to boost reader numbers, which it had done, and that had to be enough for her. Except it wasn't, Holly admitted silently as she exchanged spirited high fives with the other girls.

But hang on a minute, Holly thought as the celebration subsided. Wasn't this expansion of the column and securing of their jobs the moment she'd been working towards? And wasn't it essential to immerse herself in that work if she was going to forget being anxious about supper with Signor Sexy tonight? Her gaze fired as the other girls looked to her expectantly. 'Chocolate?' she said.

'Tick!' the girls chorused.

'Bottle of fizz to celebrate?' She was less sure of this one and was already planning to slip out and buy something.

'Tick!' Pixie said triumphantly, producing a bottle from behind her back.

'I think we have everything we need,' Holly confirmed. 'Let's kick this column into shape!'

And let me have something I *can* control to think about, she prayed fervently, instead of a whole lot of man that I can't.

# CHAPTER FIVE

*'Mirror, mirror on the wall—' Will someone cover the damn mirror!*

*Tonight's the night. I am taking the playboy out to supper and I can't decide what to wear.*

*I realise that taking him out reverses the natural order of things—but then I am not the playboy's natural order, if you take my meaning. I am more of a meagre side dish—the type of thing you order to try, and more often than not leave untouched.*

*Me? Lacking in confidence? What makes you think that?*

*All right. I admit it. Every item of clothing I possess is on the bed, or on the floor. Carrier bags and sales tickets are scattered around like confetti, because, as it turns out, my wardrobe is full of nothing to wear. And, as I am constantly reminded by the playboy's long-legged basquewearing friends, sex sells. Not exactly my area of expertise. Consequently, I have decided that my next article for you will be a helpful piece on the subject of staying out of debt. At least that's where my credit card provider told me I should be concentrating my thoughts.*

*I must admit the real crisis of confidence came*

*when I tried to decide what to underpin my modest outfit with tonight. As I don't possess a single basque, or hold-up stocking, should I chance a shocking-pink thong?*

*As my underwear is unlikely to receive an airing, that hardly matters, does it?*

*And the playboy? He's acting as cool and as sexy as ever. Accompanying me to supper is nothing more than a workaday chore for him in order to keep in his sister's good books. So at least I should be safe. And I should be glad about that—right?*

TYPING up her column was a displacement activity Holly had hoped would take her mind off the fact that she would soon be sitting across a table from Ruiz—speaking to him, staring into his eyes—all the time pretending they were nothing more than friends. Her shopping had been more erratic than usual with her frantic purchases more suitable for a royal wedding than a casual supper in a local bistro and she was fast losing confidence in her ability to pull this off.

Closing the lid on her laptop, Holly glanced at the shoe box the unscrupulous Ruiz had left temptingly outside her door. It was on her bed now. She had been forced to bring it into the bedroom in case someone fell over it. But of course she couldn't wear the shoes unless Ruiz allowed her to pay for them. And as that would take a whole month's salary...

The dress she had finally chosen to wear was a sale-rail spectacular—A-line, with a flirty skirt and a high scooped neck. It wasn't black, which was about the best that could be said for it, but at least it was the same soft blue as her favourite shirt. With her hair neatly brushed, lip gloss present and correct, and just a suggestion of smudgy grey eye shadow to complement the flick of black mascara, she was ready. And nervous.

What did she have to be nervous about? Eating supper was a harmless activity.

Sharing food could be very sexy.

Fish and chips?

Mating rituals like eating supper together and how to avoid them was another good headline for her column, Holly concluded as she shifted anxiously from foot to foot in the hallway, waiting for Ruiz. But seeing as there was no escape from tonight, fish was out—ditto anything like spinach that might get stuck in her teeth. Thankfully, she had identified a healthy-food café where they could nibble on crudités and drink sparkling elder-flower water. Perfect. She would keep a clear head and as the café was brilliantly lit with sensible, hard-backed chairs Ruiz wouldn't want to stay for long—

*And when they came home?*

She'd plead tiredness and go to bed. Alone.

Just when she'd almost given up on him, Ruiz stormed back into the apartment like an avenging angel in a cloud of cold air and warm smiles with Bouncer panting vigorously at his heels. 'Ready?' he demanded.

'Ready,' Holly confirmed.

'Where are you taking me?' he said as he bent down to remove Bouncer's leash.

'I thought the little café down the road—'

'The one where we met?' Ruiz sounded upbeat as his lips pressed down with approval of her choice. 'Hang on while I fill Bouncer's water bowl—'

'No… No, that one's shut,' she called out.

Ruiz sauntered back into the hall. 'Tell me you're not taking me to that place where they serve lentil soup, and you have to sit round a communal table on hemp sacks?'

'What's wrong with that?' she said. 'They do have private booths.'

'Where you can sit on even bigger hemp sacks? No, thank you.'

'So where do you want to go?' she said irritably.

'You're letting me choose?' Ruiz's mouth curved in a grin.

Why couldn't she learn to keep her big mouth shut? She would never be able to afford Ruiz's preferred style of restaurant. 'I'm sure I can find somewhere else you would like,' she told him firmly.

'I know somewhere you'd like,' Ruiz countered. 'It's walking distance from here—and not expensive,' he added when Holly's eyes widened in panic. 'Mid-week is all about economy, Ms Valiant.'

'Are you mocking me, Señor Acosta?'

'Would I?' he said.

Holly's look said it all. And now her mind was swinging wildly between the safe café of her choice and somewhere of Ruiz's choosing—and how *economical* that would be in terms of their very different incomes. 'Am I dressed okay for this place of yours?'

'You'll do,' he said, holding her gaze with a raised eyebrow and a sexy grin.

'It's still my treat,' she insisted firmly, trying to hang onto her composure.

'Of course it is,' Ruiz agreed. 'Though I am prepared to make a deal with you.'

Why was he staring at her shoes? Her comfortable, clunky-heeled shoes? They were perfect if they were going to walk to the place Ruiz had mentioned. Did he need to look at them as if she had committed some terrible faux pas and make her even more nervous about stepping into Ruiz's world than she already was?

'This is the deal.' Ruiz angled his disreputably stubbled chin in Holly's direction. 'I'll pay for supper tonight if you wear the shoes I bought for you.'

The shoes he bought? Accept his gift? Take a totter on the wild side on five-inch heels instead of remaining safely corralled inside the magazine column on her clunkies? 'I can't walk in high heels. And, anyway, I already told you that I—'

'Don't accept gifts from men,' Ruiz supplied. 'I do remember.'

'So, how does this work?' Holly demanded. 'I get the shoes and you pay for supper. Do you seriously think I'm going to go for that?'

'I think you should,' he said evenly. 'I think if you had any sense you would.'

'Well, clearly I don't have any sense,' Holly fired back, 'because—' Because what? Come on, come on '—because tonight is supposed to be my treat for you.' Ah, yes, sweet relief. 'Because you have to let me do something in return for allowing me to stay in the Acosta penthouse.' *Yes!* 'And as for wearing a pair of brand-new shoes that you could easily take back to the store and get a refund for—'

'Oh, get over yourself,' Ruiz flashed, raising the emotional temperature by a few thousand degrees. 'You're my sister's best friend. If my friends were in London and needed accommodation I would expect Lucia to show them hospitality. This is a courtesy to my sister.'

As she had thought. Okay, she'd asked for that, Holly accepted as Ruiz and his storm-face reached the door. 'Okay?' he questioned, banging it open.

'Okay,' she fired back. Stepping out of the fictional world she had created for Ruiz and into reality with him might be a little more combative and complex than she had first imagined, Holly realised. And as for the effect on her senses, she could only trust that the keeper of her moral code was on duty tonight.

'I thought we might go dancing,' Ruiz dropped in casually as he held the door for her to go through.

'Dancing?' Holly managed on a dry throat, knowing her face must have been a picture of doom as she walked past him.

'Something wrong with that?' Ruiz demanded, turning to lock the door.

Where to start? Dancing meant touching each other, holding each other, moving as closely as two people could move together, unless they were—

'Those shoes are perfect for dancing. Thank you for wearing them,' Ruiz said with worrying charm as she click-clacked across the lobby towards the elevator.

'My pleasure,' Holly said primly, which was the understatement of the year. Well, she could hardly leave the shoes alone in a box while she went out, could she? They might fade, or something.

'Tonight should make very good reading for your column,' Ruiz observed as they stood waiting for the lift to arrive.

Holly forced a small laugh. Not too good, she hoped. She'd given up on the thong and was wearing really big knickers instead.

They crossed the road and walked through the park with a good three feet of air between them. Where was Ruiz taking her? Holly wondered as he turned off down a cobbled side street where the mews houses would go for millions and any club would be exclusive in the extreme. She was feeling extremely self-conscious by the time Ruiz stopped outside an iron-studded door where the faint strains of South American music could be heard on the street. But the club did look intriguing—all dark and mysterious like the man at her side.

'A Brazilian friend of mine owns the club,' Ruiz explained. 'They have great food and even better dancing. A place like this will be dynamite for your column. Ready, Holly?'

As she would ever be, Holly thought, taking a deep breath.

When would she get another chance like this? Holly asked herself sensibly. The humour in Ruiz's eyes reassured her, though when he rested his arm across her shoulders as they waited for the doorman to examine their faces through the grill, she had to tell herself that Ruiz was just doing his thing and that it was in his nature to make people feel good.

Richly carpeted steps led down to a luxurious, stone-flagged basement, where lead-paned glass glinted in the sultry glow of candles. The heavy polished furniture and rich draperies in ruby reds and regal purples gave the club an established sense of luxury and indulgence. Ruiz was right about it providing food for her column. It was not only packed, she could see now through the archway leading into the main dining room and dance floor, but, judging by the clientele, it was the hottest place in town. Her readers would definitely be interested, Holly thought as Ruiz held her coat. 'Is that a samba they're playing?'

'Very good,' Ruiz remarked as he handed Holly's coat to an attendant. 'I can tell you're eager to dance—'

'Oh, no,' Holly exclaimed as her pulse raced off the scale. 'I'm only here to observe.' But in her head she was already practising the steps. She had taken some classes a while back with a friend, but her heart thundered at the thought that Ruiz might put her to the test. She reassured herself that the samba had been one of the easiest dances to learn: *back, forward, forward.* There were only three steps to remember, for goodness' sake—

'You do dance the samba…?'

Ruiz's eyes were dancing with laughter, Holly noticed. 'And how do you know that?' she challenged him.

'You're mouthing the steps.'

'No, I'm not,' Holly argued, relieved when the maître d' arrived to escort them to their table. He had seated them right at the edge of the dance floor, which was fantastic for watching the dancers, but terrible if, like Holly, you didn't want to be so dangerously close to the action.

'The steps will soon come back to you,' Ruiz assured her with an amused smile.

'I'm sure you're right,' Holly agreed as the maitre d' removed the reserved sign with a flourish.

'And I think you're going to be very good at it,' Ruiz prompted when Holly gave him a look. 'Dancing, I mean.'

As Ruiz lounged back in his comfortably padded chair all Holly could think about was the scary dance teacher, yelling at her to *Bounce, Valiant, bounce! For goodness' sake, lift your feet, girl!* Before she fell over them presumably. Would samba lessons delivered in her local community centre by a moustachioed teacher help her now? Holly wondered as she gazed at the slinky couples moving effortlessly around the floor. Somehow, she doubted it. This samba was faster, cooler, and way sexier than she remembered, especially when she compared it to her shambling attempts. But then she had been dancing with an equally uncoordinated girl. Men had been thin on the ground in the classes, so most of the women ended up dancing together, Holly remembered, glanc-

ing at her rugged companion. Dancing with Ruiz Acosta
might be somewhat different, she suspected.

He was impatient when people kept on greeting him—
especially impatient when he noticed the curious glances
they were lavishing on Holly. He should have known better than to bring her here but he had wanted her to have a
treat. He had wanted to get her away from the computer
and from the shadows of the past for just one evening. He
would have liked half an hour with the man who hurt her.
She was so inexperienced, so vulnerable. He hated the
type of man who took advantage of that. He wondered
if Holly had ever known love. Lucia had told him something about her clever friend who had been sent away to
school on a scholarship by parents who never visited. No
wonder his generous-hearted sister had palled up with
sensible Holly Valiant. He could see it all now. Lucia had
provided the warmth Holly had so badly needed, while
Holly had kept his sister in line—just about.

'What are you smiling at now?' she said.

'Thinking about Lucia…'

'Ah.' She relaxed.

'And I'm enjoying myself,' he confessed, only realising now how true that was. He was completely relaxed—
especially now that everyone had taken the hint and seen
that he wanted to be alone with his supper companion.
Had anyone ever made love to Holly, he wondered, or
had they just used her without ever seeing the side of her
that Holly kept so close? She was different from anyone
he had ever known. He knew most women only wanted
him for the material things he could provide—things in
which Holly had absolutely no interest.

'Do you mind if I take my shoes off?' she said, distracting him from his thoughts as she pulled a comic

face. 'I'll keep my feet under the table so you don't have to look at them—'

He laughed as she kicked the expensive shoes he'd bought her into touch.

She watched Ruiz greet acquaintances with a casual wave. He knew a lot of people in London, or, rather, a lot of people knew Ruiz, Holly amended, and they all seemed inordinately pleased if he noticed them. Perhaps it was she who needed a wake-up call, Holly reflected. Ruiz was an international sportsman and highly respected—

'Are you okay?' Ruiz prompted.

'Of course.'

'I want you to enjoy yourself.'

'I'm sure I shall.' She thought about Ruiz's comment regarding entertaining friends of the family and hoped she wasn't keeping him from his own friends. 'It's very good of you to bring me here,' she said politely.

Ruiz gave her a quizzical look. 'It's very good of you to come with me.'

Was it? Even in jeans and a crisp white shirt Ruiz looked amazing and exuded class, while Holly was increasingly aware of buying something just because it was in the sale that really didn't suit her and that was now clinging unattractively to her bargain-basement body.

'Would you like to dance?' Ruiz suggested.

'With you?'

'Were you thinking of dancing with someone else?' he queried with a sultry growl.

'In front of everyone?'

'That is the usual way.'

'Won't people talk? So many people seem to know who you are.'

'And if they do?'

'I don't want you to be unmasked,' Holly whispered dramatically, thinking she had found the perfect excuse not to dance with the playboy in public.

'Do they give you a byline on the Playboy column these days?' Ruiz asked innocently.

'No, of course they don't put my name on the column. I'm part of a team—'

*Stop!* Stop Talking NOW, Holly's inner voice advised, before you dig the hole any deeper. Of course no one knew who she was. She was just another of Ruiz's many female friends as far as the people at the club were concerned. 'Shall we chat and eat first?' she suggested, red-faced.

For a moment she thought Ruiz would argue and insist on dancing, but he just said, 'Whatever you like,' and picked up the menu.

And now she was disappointed. A hemp sack and a bowl of lentils was pretty much what she deserved, Holly concluded. Burying her head in the menu, she mentally revisited the conversation where Ruiz had made it clear that this evening was all about entertaining his sister's friend.

'Are you going to relax any time soon, Holly?'

She looked up. 'I'm sorry. I'm just a bit overwhelmed by all this.'

'All this?'

'I feel a bit out of place here, to be honest.' Whereas Ruiz was so confident and so good-looking he was at ease anywhere.

'Out of place? Why should you say that? I can't think of anyone who deserves a night off more than you do, Holly. Since the moment I met you, you've been working all hours.'

'But all these people are so—' She snatched a breath as Ruiz's hand touched her arm.

'Choose something to eat,' he prompted.

Studying the menu, and actually reading it this time, Holly gulped when she saw the prices. When the waiter arrived to take their order she told him that a starter-sized salad would be enough for her. Shaking his head, Ruiz countermanded that idea and ordered for her. 'You don't have to eat what I've ordered for you,' he explained, 'but if you're going to continue working at the pace you do, one lettuce leaf and a spoonful of dressing isn't enough to keep you going.'

Ruiz's amused glance lasted a little longer this time and as she held it something told Holly that if she could relax they might be friends. After all, Ruiz was her best friend's brother, and she loved Lucia…

The meal Ruiz had ordered for Holly was delicious. He had chosen perfectly. The most delicious halibut she had ever tasted came with side orders of buttered spinach, roasted tomatoes, and creamy mashed potatoes. Ruiz devoured an epic steak, and after the meal they drank strong, aromatic coffee as they watched professional dancers giving an eye-popping demonstration of how the samba should be danced. Surely, Ruiz couldn't expect her to do that? Holly thought, imagining how she might interpret the hip grinding and pelvic thrusting, which the professional dancers managed to turn into something so erotic, and yet so stylish. It might look rather different if she took to the floor. And then there were the outfits. The woman's costume was glittery and filmy, barely a whisper of aquamarine chiffon decorated with diamanté, while the man's black trousers might have been sprayed on—

'And now we dance,' Ruiz announced when the applause had died down.

'I don't think so,' Holly protested, sitting deeper in her chair.

Ruiz gave her no option. Making her gasp as he lifted her out of the seat, he lowered her onto a dance floor crowded with couples only too eager to show what they could do. 'You can't force me,' Holly protested, turning to go.

'And you can't resist the music.' He brought her back again.

Short of drawing attention to herself, she had no option but to go through the motions of dancing one samba, Holly concluded. She was just gearing herself up to do this when another man, crowned with the same menacing glamour as Ruiz, strode up to them. Swinging a welcoming arm around Ruiz's shoulders, he exclaimed, 'Hello, my friend. Long time no see.' His gaze remained fixed on Holly's face—assessing and no doubt drawing all the wrong conclusions, she thought. This must be the Brazilian friend Ruiz had told her about, Holly concluded as the two men exchanged a fierce hug.

Ruiz confirmed this when he introduced them. 'Holly, I'd like you to meet an old friend and adversary of mine—'

'Not so much of the old, please,' Gabriel insisted with his gaze still trained on Holly. 'Though I won't argue about our adversarial tendencies.'

'Gabriel,' Holly said politely, hoping she wouldn't get her hand scorched off when she shook his hand. Was there a whole contingent of stunning South Americans living in London? Holly wondered as more, equally striking men joined their group.

'Polo players,' Ruiz explained, slipping out of Portuguese

with Gabriel into Spanish with some of the others. 'My apologies, Holly,' he added politely. 'We will speak only English now,' Ruiz instructed his friends.

Polo players? She would never have guessed, Holly mused wryly, taking in the muscular physiques. All the men looked like athletes and none of them was afraid of staring her straight in the eyes. She wasn't used to such forthright inspection and felt her cheeks fire red. And then Ruiz introduced her by explaining that Holly was an agony aunt, which only brought a fresh blood-rush to her cheeks.

'Holly doesn't look much like your auntie to me,' Gabriel commented dryly.

'If *you* need any help or advice, Holly, don't hesitate to call me,' another man drawled.

'Enough,' Ruiz commanded good-humouredly. To Holly's further amazement, he then placed a protective arm around her shoulders. 'You'll have Holly believing all South Americans are best avoided by respectable women.'

'Respectable women?' Gabriel commented in a low drawl. 'Now there's a rare breed. You must allow me to offer you the hospitality of my club,' Gabriel added, switching his amused, worldly stare from Holly's face to Ruiz. 'At least for the first part of your evening. The rest of the night is up, to you my friends.'

'That's enough, Gabe.' Ruiz cautioned his friend in a low voice in a way that made Holly feel unusually protected.

Not a bad feeling, she concluded, if one she was unused to. Ruiz leaping to her defence was surprise enough, but seeing how quickly the other men backed off when he told them to communicated a lot about Ruiz. 'Thank you,' she said quietly when they were alone again.

'For what?' Ruiz demanded.

'I think you know,' she said.

# CHAPTER SIX

*Playing with fire and the consequences thereof.
Someone once told me that dancing is one of the
few things we humans do in perfect rhythm with a
partner, and that the other notable activity, more
often than not, follows afterwards.
Fat chance, is all I can say.
Oh, and I would write at greater length, but tapping away under the table while the playboy briefly
chats with more admirers doesn't give me much
chance to wax lyrical. I can only say that the consequences of the gawkiest redhead in town attend-
ing the hottest club in town with the sexiest man in
town, steeling herself to dance the hottest dance on
the planet with a man born to move in rhythm with
a partner, should give you a laugh—*

HER next column would be one heck of a read, Holly
concluded as Ruiz led her onto the dance floor. Seeing
him here outside an environment they shared was interesting. She liked him better if anything. The respect
Ruiz attracted from the other men was a measure of
him, and although she was the clumsiest thing on two
feet she felt confident Ruiz would never laugh at her or
put her down the way her ex had. She only had to see

him with his friends to know Ruiz was all about making people feel good.

'Please excuse my friends,' he said as if he had picked up on her thoughts. 'Waiting for the polo season to get underway frustrates them. I'm afraid they're suffering an overdose of testosterone without the opportunity to work it off.'

'I'm really not that sensitive.'

'In the workplace? I would agree with you,' he said. 'But personally…I'm not so sure.'

'They really didn't upset me,' Holly stressed. 'So *you* can relax.'

'If you ask me to…'

As his lips tugged she shivered with awareness. What was the female equivalent of Ruiz's friends' problem? Pheromone-frenzy? Whatever it might be she had it bad.

'We're all impatient for the polo season to start, Holly,' Ruiz confided, drawing her gaze back to his strong, dark face.

Her name sounded so exotic on Ruiz's lips it must be way past the time to steer her thoughts onto safer ground. 'You must miss polo and Argentina very much.'

'I miss my brothers more than the game. I even miss that wretched sister of mine,' Ruiz admitted wryly. 'I miss the space and the wild free gallops,' he added, drawing her close, fortunately so engaged in his own thoughts Ruiz missed her sharp intake of breath as she collided with his hard body. 'And I miss the warmth of the people.'

There was quite a lot of warmth going on here too, Holly thought as Ruiz pressed against her, but then she noticed he was staring over her head at nothing in particular, as if his thoughts were somewhere else, far away. But when the music started to play and his hand found hers she thrilled at the warmth of his touch. He moved gently at first, easing her into the dance, his confident movements in perfect timing with the beat of the music. He held her so lightly, and yet the music seemed to flow from him to her so that even Holly's awkward body responded perfectly. She was infected by the rhythm, and by Ruiz, Holly concluded, and by the sense that on a cold winter's night there was nowhere else on earth she would rather be than dancing the samba in Ruiz's arms.

Had she gone completely mad?

Probably, Holly thought as Ruiz, having told her to relax, firmed his grip. 'That's better,' he approved as she began to move a little more confidently to the music, but then he added, 'I think you have been less than honest with me, Holly.'

'What do you mean?' Her head shot up.

'You can dance,' Ruiz said, smiling.

She smiled back, feeling good inside. Her hand felt right in his, and with Ruiz's arm around her waist, his fingers lightly holding her, she realised she liked being part of a couple—this couple—however fleeting this chance of being with Ruiz might be. They moved well together, easily, as if they had been dancing this way all their lives. She had never made a show of herself like this before, yet here she was, dancing in public with a man born to use his body expertly, while she was twirling and flirting with her hips and with her eyes—

What was the worst that could happen? She could make a fool of herself? Something told her Ruiz would never allow that to happen.

'You're not even treading on my feet,' he said dryly, dipping his head to direct this observation with a smile into her eyes.

'Nor you on mine,' she agreed.

'Unusual for me,' Ruiz remarked, smiling wickedly again.

She loved it when he teased her. She loved... Unfortunately for her peace of mind, she loved most things about Ruiz.

The samba was fast and flirty. If she had chosen to represent each of them with a dance it would be the passionate tango for Ruiz and an energetic barn dance with more gusto than panache for Holly. But somehow they were meeting in the middle with this highly charged, fast-moving pas de deux that left her little time to wonder if she was doing it right. No time to think, no time to feel self-conscious. Just fun and laughter, flashing eyes, and moving her body to the rhythm of the music in a way she wouldn't have believed possible until tonight.

'Now you're really getting into it,' Ruiz approved as he spun her round.

'You know I'm only doing my best to keep up.'

'No. You have a natural flair,' Ruiz insisted, drawing her close again.

'Not really. There are some great dancers here.' And Ruiz was one of them, as every woman in the club seemed to agree. Thank goodness he couldn't see her face, Holly thought as she relished the unaccustomed sensation of being pressed up close against him. Tough, hard and strong, Ruiz might look like a swarthy bad boy on the rampage, but he moved like a dream.

And this was a man whose reputation made Casanova seem like a choir boy. And what had happened the last time she had allowed herself to be lulled into a trance-like state by a good-looking man? Images of half-empty wine bottles and crisp packets piled up on a carpet of chocolate wrappers crowded into her head. Did she really want to go back there? Not that Ruiz had any need of her money.

'I've lost you,' he chided as the dance floor began to clear. 'Where are you now, Holly? Worrying about the steps for the next dance?' he suggested as the music started up again.

There couldn't be a next dance if she wanted to keep any sense of reality where Ruiz was concerned. Her less than platonic feelings for him could only mean she was setting herself up for a fall. 'Shouldn't we be getting back for Bouncer?'

'The dog?' Ruiz gave her one of his looks. 'Didn't I take him out for the longest walk ever before we came here?'

'He has been on his own for rather a long time.'

'And will be asleep by now, I have no doubt,' Ruiz assured her, his sexy eyes darkening in a smile. And then the infectious beat started up again. The moment his hand found the hollow in the small of her back she was lost. They were good together—frighteningly good.

When the dance ended Ruiz held her at arm's length. 'I don't know when I've enjoyed myself so much, Holly.'

Was he serious? The adrenalin rush that had been brought on by dancing with Ruiz was subsiding, leaving a gap for Holly's self-esteem issues to fill.

'Thank you for tonight,' he said.

'I won't put your toes in danger again, I promise.'

'Where are you going?' Ruiz caught hold of her.

'To get my coat. To call a taxi.' She held up her hand when Ruiz seemed as if he might argue with her. 'You don't have to leave. Thank you for a wonderful evening, Ruiz.'

Dipping his head low, Ruiz stared into her eyes. 'Do

you think I'm going to let you call a cab and leave the club on your own?'

'I'm not a baby, Ruiz. And you don't have to spoil your night just because I'm going home.'

'I brought you here. I'm taking you home. And, anyway, it's too late for you to be out on your own.'

If Ruiz was talking about the dangers of the night he would come top of her list. 'I'll be fine in a cab,' Holly insisted. 'If it makes you feel better, why don't you call a reputable company of your own choosing?'

She was serious, he realised. He had to admire Holly's strength of will. She was an independent woman and he respected that, but all he could think was how she'd felt in his arms when they danced together and how he didn't want the evening to end. Holly was all woman—she just didn't know it yet. Her hair had felt like spun silk beneath his hands and her body was— Now who was writing up a storm? 'I'm taking you home,' he said firmly, flashing a warning glance at his friends who had been viewing their little altercation from the bar.

She slept with Bouncer that night. Much safer. And as far as *sex sells* went, how about a snuffly dog with an ear-splitting snore? How well would that sell? 'Oh, Bouncer,' Holly complained softly as the big dog began to chase rabbits in his sleep. 'I can see I'm not going to get any more rest tonight.'

Retrieving the duvet from the floor where Bouncer had kicked it, Holly glanced at the clock on the wall. Three a.m. Great. There was only one thing for it—she might as well start writing her next column. It wasn't as if she didn't have anything to say. Creeping out of the bedroom, she sat down at her usual place in the living room and began to write, and write. She soon had enough to fill a double-paged spread. Pausing for thought, she started thundering on the keyboard again, hardly realising that she was reasoning out her feelings for Ruiz—

*The playboy is the youngest of a notorious band of polo-playing brothers and also the brother of my best friend, so of course we have a bond. He is someone I can be friends with, but nothing more—even if he wanted more, which, obviously, he doesn't...*

'Don't stop now—'

Holly swung round in shock to find Ruiz, barefoot in a black tee and boxers, standing behind her, blatantly reading her screen.

'I was just enjoying that,' he protested as she shut the lid on her laptop.

Her cheeks fired with embarrassment. 'Don't you have any manners?'

'In the bedroom? Yes. In the office? No. This is your temporary office, isn't it, Holly?' And then, as if such a wealth of tan and muscle on so broad-shouldered a frame weren't enough to scramble her brains completely, he leaned low to murmur, 'We really have to stop meeting like this...'

'I couldn't agree more,' she said primly, refusing absolutely to acknowledge the way Ruiz was making her feel.

'Can I get you a drink?' he said. 'Hot milk, perhaps? Or cocoa?'

'You can stop teasing me,' she warned. Standing, she drew herself up to her full five feet three, which only succeeded in amusing Ruiz as she had to lean back to look him in the eye. But then she thought about what he'd said. 'Am I really so boring that you think I need hot milk?'

'I wouldn't call you boring.' Ruiz's sexy mouth pressed down in wry conjecture as he pretended to think about it. 'Irritating, maybe—'

'Like an itch you can't reach?' she suggested dryly.

'Oh, I can reach you,' Ruiz assured her softly.

Not quite so sure she wanted to play this game any longer, Holly watched warily as Ruiz walked towards her. She couldn't have been more surprised when he leaned forward to brush a kiss against her lips. Without meaning to, she swayed against him. He moved away.

'See you in the morning, Holly.'

She stared after him, deciding her readers would never know what a close call she'd had.

Tactics that had worked so well for him in the past didn't work with Holly. And he wouldn't want them to, Ruiz concluded as he directed a frustrated punch at his pillow. Was she still working? Was she asleep? Closing his eyes, he tried running the company balance sheets in his head. That had always worked for him in the past, but not tonight, because tonight all he could see was Holly in overlarge pyjamas with her bare feet crossed and tucked neatly beneath the chair while she sat with her head bowed over her laptop, feverishly tapping away.

'Ruiz?'

He shot up.

'I'm sorry to disturb you,' Holly murmured as she opened the door just a crack. 'Bouncer was begging to go out and now he seems to have hurt his paw in the garden.'

'You went outside at night on your own?' He was half-way across the room by this time. 'Don't do that again,' he said, striding past Holly towards the kitchen.

'I didn't have much choice,' Holly insisted, catching up with him. 'I bathed the paw,' she explained as he hunkered down to take a look.

'I can't see anything,' he admitted.

'Neither could I. Maybe he trod on some glass? He was limping when he came back into the kitchen.'

'Did you give him a biscuit when you brought him in?'

'Why, yes, I did,' Holly admitted. 'And once I was sure he was okay I gave him another to reassure him.'

Ruiz grinned as he ruffled the big dog's fur. 'That's one of Bouncer's favourite tricks—limping, and then the hangdog expression. Works every time, doesn't it, boy?'

'He had me,' Holly admitted ruefully, shooting Bouncer a hard stare. 'I'm really sorry for getting you out of bed, Ruiz, especially as it looks like it was for nothing.'

'Better safe than sorry,' he observed, springing up.

He realised then how tiny Holly was in bare feet, and how big and clumsy he was by comparison. More concerning was the fact that he was only wearing boxers and a tee. 'You're not going back to work, are you?' he asked as she turned for the door.

'Maybe—I keep a personal diary too. Remember? I told you. Always have,' she explained.

And wouldn't he love to see that! 'How does anyone find the time?'

'Only child?'

'Ah, yes. Lucia told me. No siblings to distract you.' He realised then that Holly must have had plenty of time to record her thoughts, and that what had been a hobby to begin with had become a habit now. 'So what was it like having my sister as a friend at boarding school?' he asked curiously, not wanting Holly to go just yet.

She laughed. 'Quite a shock to my system. I was an only child used to doing what I was told.'

'And Lucia was a very different animal?' Ruiz's lips tugged. He understood.

How had she become best friends with the most attractive and outgoing girl in the school? Thinking back, Holly remembered Lucia not just being high spirited and up to mischief half of the time, but so incredibly warm, and interested in everyone—not unlike her brother, Ruiz. It was a tribute both to their good nature and to their brother Nacho, who had brought them up.

'Lucia and I made quite a team,' she explained. 'We egged each other on and skated a very thin line between total exclusion from the school and one of our crazy ideas taking off. Lucky for us, one of our ideas worked so well we managed to get a whole pile of money from a government educational grant to develop our ecological project.'

'Was that where the green hair came in?'

'Are you accusing me of deliberately dying my hair green?'

'Should I be?' Ruiz said wryly.

'It may have had something to do with it.'

'So, in summary you were both holy terrors?'

'You don't know the half,' Holly agreed.

'Which is perhaps just as well,' Ruiz commented, his ruggedly handsome face creasing in a rueful grin. 'Well. I suppose I should turn in. Thanks for looking after our mutual friend.'

'Don't you want some ice cream?'

'Ice cream?'

'When it's this late and you don't want to start eating proper food again, ice cream fills a gap, I find.'

'Does it?' Ruiz said in a tone that made her toes curl. She was already rifling through the freezer box by this time, shaking convulsively and not with cold. She had never led a man on before. But this was new Holly, and there was a first time for everything...

Holly licked her lips when she found the carton of ice cream she was looking for. He realised then that had any other woman done that he would have interpreted the request as she would have wanted him to, but with Holly it was different. She was different. Meanwhile, Bouncer might not be the talking dog, but the big mutt had a very eloquent way of expressing himself. Currently stretched out in a contented sprawl snoring softly, Bouncer had clearly forgotten all thoughts of sore paws and looked as if everything in his world was going to plan.

Ruiz took up every available inch in the kitchen. There was no way past his bed-ruffled, barely clad form unless he backed out of her way. Stretching up, she tried reaching for two bowls, then, spotting something else, she changed her mind and grabbed a pack of ice-cream cornets instead. But now her hand was shaking so much she couldn't get the ice-cream scoop to connect with the contents of the tub.

'Here, let me help you with that,' Ruiz offered. 'If we put the scoop in boiling water first—' He stopped. 'Holly? You're really shaking. Are you cold?'

'Yes,' she exclaimed, grabbing the cue Ruiz had given her like a life raft. Could desire do this to you? She had no idea what desire could do, having never felt anything to compare with this before. With her ex she had been so pathetically grateful that he noticed her at all that her own passion had never really come into it. She had been too busy trying to please him, to keep him, to keep his interest—

'Why don't you turn the heating up, while I serve the ice cream?' Ruiz suggested, sounding as normal as ever, as if two people clad in nightclothes—one of them barely clad at all—could have a companionable chat in the middle of the night without feeling as incredibly aware as she did. Could she squeeze past him without touching? She glanced at the climate control on the wall, knowing she wasn't even remotely cold, but it was too late to admit that now.

'Come on,' Ruiz prompted, pressing his muscular form back against the side to let her past.

Was he kidding? This was a really bad idea. She was hardly experienced enough to play flirting games with Ruiz, let alone rub past so much muscle. But she would have to...

Sucking in her stomach, she braced herself. Avoiding contact was impossible. Ruiz tried to help, but she still got stuck. 'This is a tight squeeze,' he observed dryly.

She tried to reach over him to the control, conscious all the time of his hot, hard, naked thigh pressed up against her. 'You're taking up all the space. I can't reach anything. You'll have to move.'

*Please, please move—*

Ruiz didn't move a muscle. 'I thought you said you needed warming up?' he commented.

'I do—' Her hand flailed about searching for the elusive heat control, while her gaze never left Ruiz's dark, amused stare. He might well look like that when her body had somehow moulded itself around his without any input from her at all.

'Shall we forget about the ice cream?' he asked.

Her breath hitched in her throat as Ruiz dipped his

head towards her, but she had called it wrong. Instead of kissing her, as she had thought he might, he dabbled ice cream on her cheek. Exclaiming with surprise, she pushed him away. 'You—!'

Ruiz seized her wrist and drew her close. 'Don't wipe it off,' he said, frowning. 'What a waste…' She trembled uncontrollably as he moved her hand away and licked the ice cream from her face. She was still reeling from this when he dabbed some more on her neck. 'This is delicious,' he observed as coolly as if they were sharing a meal in a café.

Sweet sensation streamed through her veins, making her more reckless and excited. She reached one hand out, cautiously feeling for the tub, but Ruiz saw what she was doing and dodged out of her way, and the best she could manage was a glancing blow to his cheek. 'How's your temperature?' she demanded, backing away to a safe distance.

'Red hot,' Ruiz assured her.

# CHAPTER SEVEN

*Have you ever felt that you were about to do something you might regret and yet were utterly powerless to stop yourself? Well, that's where I am now. I could do with a gang of you turning up at the penthouse to drag me back from the lustful brink. But I should warn you that if you do I might not be all that pleased to see you.*

*Tomorrow's another day? Yes, and I might need a hug by then. Maybe I'll know what sex can be like when you choose the right man, but we all know that for every good thing that happens there's the flip side of the coin, so I could be about to make the biggest mistake of my life.*

*And the playboy? The reason I'm telling you this is because there's a look in his eyes I haven't seen before, and after months of telling myself I don't need men I suddenly thought, Do I want to spend the rest of my life wondering what I've missed?*

COULD she remember all that? She could hardly race to the laptop now. 'The writer of this column is otherwise engaged and seems likely to be so for quite some time' was one heck of a headline, but was this moment something she wanted to share with the world? 'How is it possible I'm covered in ice cream while you have a magic ring of protection around you?' Holly demanded excitedly, playing for time. She shrieked as Ruiz prowled closer, while he just grinned and shrugged.

Why was she out of ammunition? Holly's chaotic thoughts refused to assemble into a coherent form as she backed away. It wasn't a fresh tub of ice cream she needed, but a long, cold shower and a few miles' distance between them. What had she been thinking? That she could play games with Ruiz and there would be no consequences? 'Okay. I give up.' She raised her hands in defeat. 'You're better at this than I am—'

'What do you expect with three brothers and a sister? I've been having food fights since I could lift a spoon.'

An only child could only dream of having this much fun, but at least Ruiz had ceased hostilities for now. She breathed a sigh of relief as she tried to retrieve a blob of ice cream that had landed on her chest before it could trickle any lower. But this brief pause in the ice-cream war didn't mean she liked losing. Sneakily reaching for the tub, she launched a counter attack, and, though Ruiz had the reflexes of a fighter pilot, she managed to score a hit on his mouth.

'You'll pay for that,' he warned, wiping his lips with the back of his hand.

Holly sincerely hoped so. The fears that had haunted her for so long had been consumed in the fire burning in Ruiz's eyes. It was enough to make anyone hot and reckless. She held her breath as he prowled closer. Seconds ticked away and then they both launched an attack at the same moment. A fast and furious battle ensued. Ruiz was so much stronger and faster than she was, but she was fast enough, and fiercely competitive. Everything became a blur of limbs and flying ice cream. She managed to put the island counter between them, a barricade that gave her chance to draw breath. Lifting her chin, panting and gloating, she taunted Ruiz across the gleaming stretch of granite.

He vaulted over it. 'Now what are you going to do?' he said, holding her in front of him.

She hummed, glaring at him defiantly. Struggling was pointless. Ruiz's grip was light, yet firm, while she was consumed by excitement and covered in sticky ice cream. This was hardly the moment to assume the moral high ground. Resting back in his arms, she began to laugh.

'What?' he said.

Every part of her was tingling and aware. She was free. 'Nothing you need to know,' she said, straightening up to deliver a challenging stare into Ruiz's eyes.

He had never wanted her more. His virtuous resolutions to steer clear of Lucia's friend were history. He was more interested in licking Holly clean. He kissed her cheek, her neck, tasting her, and then he tasted her some more. 'You're delicious,' he commented as she wriggled in his arms, helpless with laughter.

'And so are you—'

He wasn't prepared for her whipping up his tee, and holding it while she licked the sugared cream from his chest. He sucked in a sharp breath and his surprise didn't lessen with the look she gave him. Her eyes blazed with fire and the sort of confidence he knew was buried deep inside. 'Kiss me,' she demanded fiercely, making it sound like a challenge as she locked her hands behind his head.

A challenge? This was a pleasure. The kiss was long and hot and deep. She tasted warm and sweet, and fiercely female. There was nothing girlie, soft, or vulnerable about Holly now. This was an equal match between a woman intent on claiming her mate, and a man who rejoiced in her strength as he lifted her.

She had never done anything remotely like this before—had never clawed at a man's clothes, hungry to feel his naked body hard against her. There was nothing delicate or tender happening here. She was burning up from the inside out.

Buttons from her pyjama top flew across the kitchen and skittered across the floor as she yanked Ruiz's top over his head. He only paused briefly to protect them both, and then he took over, resting her on the side as he pushed the top from her shoulders and the pyjama pants from her legs. His clothes dropped to the floor. Excited sounds escaped her lips. Ruiz's naked torso was stronger, harder, warmer, more beautiful than even she had imagined. The wide spread of his muscular shoulders was enough to turn her on, but it was the look in his eyes that really did it for her, because that promised more excitement than she had ever known. Holding Ruiz's darkening gaze, she traced the pattern of muscle and sinew from his breastbone to his shoulder, then down over his biceps to his forearms, and on to his hands and the lean, elegant fingers. 'Now,' she whispered urgently.

He brushed his mouth against her lips—a promise that wasn't enough for her now. 'Don't tease me,' she warned him. But he did, brushing his lips and his stubble against her neck and her cheek, and then her lips, promising, always promising, yet pulling away before she could taste him. He repeated this until her body was a furnace and she was wild for him.

As Holly pressed herself against him he tested her and found her ready. He still took his time, teasing her for as long as he had with kisses. She moaned with need when he gave her the tip and then exclaimed with disappointment when he took it away again. She shivered and opened herself more for him, pressing her thighs back as he touched her, crying when he paused. He dipped again, a little deeper this time, and then retreated. She was so moist, so warm, so completely ready for him, but even with the thought of that tight wet grip waiting to claim him banging at his brain he knew it would be better for her if he made her wait.

'I can't stand this,' she raged in a shaking voice.

'You have to,' he whispered. 'It will be all the better for it—'

'Really?' she exclaimed, and, arching forward without warning, she took him. She took him. He gasped and shuddered with surprise, slammed by an overload of sensation. 'Steady,' he cautioned as her fingers bit into his buttocks. 'If you do that,' he warned as she bucked and arced against him, 'it will all be over too soon—'

She ignored him. Screaming out his name, she plunged headlong into the first climax. It was a battle to hold her in place as she thrust her hips frantically to claim each wave of pleasure as it hit her. 'You're so big,' she groaned with satisfaction as the storm subsided.

'I aim to please,' he managed to say wryly, keeping up a steady rhythm until she was ready to start again. 'I trust that wasn't a complaint,' he added in a husky whisper against her mouth, unable to resist the temptation to kiss her again.

'A complaint?' she murmured when he released her. '*I* trust that was just a sample?'

He laughed. She was ready for more and this time she didn't want any distractions. Taking him in an even firmer hold, she ground out, 'Don't tease me— Don't wait— Don't stop—'

'You're incredible,' he said. And it was true. He'd met his match.

They feasted on each other, and neither of them tired. He persuaded her to hold her thighs back so he could increase her pleasure. It was then he discovered that she loved to watch. 'You're quite something,' he murmured, accommodating that wish too. Arranging her comfortably with one leg over his shoulder and one tiny foot on the counter, he worked steadily to keep her hovering on the edge, but this was the hottest woman he'd ever known. Could *he* hold on? 'I'll tell you when,' he instructed, staring deep into her eyes.

Her retaliation was swift and fierce, 'Don't make me wait,' she warned him. 'Don't you dare make me wait—'

'Now,' he commanded, taking her with a firm, deep thrust. The sound of her voice—the language she used— all of it increased his pleasure tenfold and this time they rode the storm together, inventing a new erotic dictionary along the way.

They must have been unconscious for a few moments, Holly thought as she slowly came round to find Ruiz resting against her, breathing steadily, still holding her safe in his arms.

'What?' he murmured, raising his head to look at her.

A sudden rush of doubt swept through her at the thought of what they'd done. Without the same hunger driving her she had too much time to think.

'Holly?' Ruiz prompted, sensing the change in her.

'Nothing,' she said. But there was something wrong, and they both knew it. A game that had started out so innocently had turned into something so much more.

'Do you regret it?' Ruiz asked with concern.

'No, of course not.' Reaching up, she closed her eyes and kissed him, but the doubts refused to go away.

'You're not frightened of me, are you?' Ruiz demanded softly when they broke apart.

Nothing could be further from the truth. She wasn't frightened of Ruiz. She was frightened of her feelings for him.

Cupping her chin so she couldn't avoid his gaze, Ruiz demanded, 'Is there someone else?'

That was so ridiculous she laughed. 'There's no one else,' she exclaimed. But Ruiz was partly right, even if he was wholly wrong. She was completely here in the moment with him, but the past couldn't be erased, and she couldn't forget that when her ex had come on the scene she had been so grateful, so thrilled by the attention he lavished on her, she had fallen for it—for him— to the extent that she would have trusted him with her life. Fortunately, she had only trusted him with her bank card, but her small pot of savings had disappeared just the same. No wonder she doubted her own judgment now.

Ruiz eased her carefully down, making sure she was steady on her feet before he let her go. 'Forget him,' he said in a voice she had never heard him use before. 'Whoever he was he can't hurt you now. I won't let anyone hurt you, Holly. You have to learn from the past and move on. Don't you think you can? Why not? When we first met you weren't sure you could make it as a journalist, but look at you now. Where has that woman gone?'

'On permanent vacation?' She smiled wryly to make light of it, but Ruiz wasn't in the mood for a joke and told her so. 'It's time to give yourself a break, Holly.'

'And it's time you stopped being kind to me for your sister's sake,' she fired back, knowing even as she said it that she was allowing the past to spoil things for her.

'You think I'm being kind to you?' Ruiz said.

'What can I think when you've already told me that

being kind to me for Lucia's sake is what you feel obliged to do?'

'You're twisting my words. You should have more confidence in yourself Holly.'

She dragged in a shuddering breath as Ruiz's lips brushed her cheek and then her neck, and finally her mouth. She wanted nothing more than to believe him.

'You're still too serious,' he said, drawing back to look at her, but then his wicked mouth tugged in a smile, 'and here was me thinking I had done everything possible to make you smile.'

She huffed and relaxed a little. Everything they had shared was reflected in Ruiz's eyes. It was both arousing and terrifying.

'More ice cream?' Ruiz suggested, refusing to be drawn into her dark mood.

'You're very bad.' But her voice was trembling as Ruiz's lips brushed her neck.

'It's your turn to lick me clean,' he observed, staring down at her with a mock-stern expression on his face. 'You started this game and now you have to finish it.'

She laughed. Holly touched him in a way no other woman had. He was so acutely tuned in to her he could feel all her hopes and fears, and not for the first time wished he could meet the man who had hurt her so badly. He wanted to keep her safe—

*Safe from him?*

He brushed that thought aside as she stared at his lips. He had never felt this way before. He had always held his feelings in, knowing Nacho had had enough to contend with bringing up three brothers and a sister. Holly had always kept her feelings in—they both had; that was their bond.

'What are you thinking?' she said quietly.

That Ruiz the fixer had always managed to fix himself, but now there was Holly in the frame. 'Are you refusing to finish this game?' The heat was rising. He could see it in her eyes. He wanted Holly to forget the past with all its false promises and disappointments. 'As it's you I'll permit the use of a clean cloth rather than your tongue,' he teased. 'I realise now that licking is only for the advanced class.'

'Don't you take anything seriously?' she asked, wondering how she was supposed to resist a man whose eyes were always so warm.

Ruiz pretended to think about it. 'The health of my polo ponies? I take that sort of thing very seriously indeed. But ice cream fights?' His lips curved in a wry smile as he shook his head. 'Sorry to disappoint you, Holly.'

'What are you doing?' she said as he drew her close.

'Now I know you're not that naïve.'

'Ruiz—' That was as far as she got.

'I want you,' he said. 'What you see is what you get with me, Holly. There is no hidden agenda. And I think you want me too. Am I wrong?'

How could she deny it? Confronted by this much strength of will she might have expected to feel weak or vulnerable, but she felt neither of those things. She felt strong. The strongest man she had ever known had made her feel confident in her own right.

'Are we going to stand here all day?' he demanded, brushing his lips against her cheek and then her neck. 'Or am I going to take you to bed?'

She was on fire for him, and as Ruiz's hold softened into a caress she linked her hands behind his neck and let him lift her.

Ruiz carried her into the bedroom and laid her down

carefully on the bed. Every instant apart from him seemed like a minute, every minute an hour. She reached for him hungrily, wanting him so strongly nothing could stop this. Ruiz's kiss was like the first time all over again, and so gentle her eyes stung to think he could be so tender. She hadn't expected such reverence. She was a plain, down-to-earth woman and expected to be treated as such, but Ruiz was kissing her as if she were made of the finest glass and might shatter in his arms if he held her too tightly. 'You're beautiful,' he murmured.

'No, I'm not.'

'If I say you're beautiful you should believe me.'

'I'm far too big,' she interrupted, trying to cross her arms over her breasts.

'How can you be too big when the top of your head barely reaches my chest? And your breasts are beautiful.'

She didn't argue when Ruiz lay beside her. Or when she shivered with pleasure as he dipped his head to lave first one nipple and then the other with his tongue so skilfully she writhed urgently on the bed, instantly hungry for him. When one powerful thigh pressed against her legs she welcomed him with a sharp cry of need, responding greedily by arching against the brutal thrust of his erection, demanding release.

She might have known he'd make her wait, and now she was all the more excited, knowing what lay in store for her. He protected them both again. Protection was for the woman to think about, she remembered her ex telling her—

She must have been mad. And desperate, Holly thought as Ruiz took her in his arms. 'No more shadows,' he whispered as if he knew where her thoughts had been straying. 'You're beautiful, and I want you, Holly. It's that simple.'

Stroking the hair back from her face, he kissed her repeatedly, and when she felt the tip of his erection brush against her she almost lost control. 'Greedy,' he murmured, soothing her when she groaned with complaint. Moving on top of her, he warmed her with kisses, cupping her buttocks as he positioned her for pleasure. This was more leisurely, allowing them to relish each sensation to the full. She pressed her hands against his chest, staring up into his eyes.

'Good?' he murmured.

'So good...' Holding his gaze, she was able to share the moment when the smooth warm tip of Ruiz's erection probed delicately before withdrawing again. It was an incredible sensation, and sucked every last shuddering breath of air out of her. He repeated the action so it was like the first time every time. He was giving her a master class in foreplay with such a concentration of sensation it wasn't long before she had to thrust towards him and take him deep—and she was still astonished by the size of him.

'How about we take it more slowly?' Ruiz suggested with amusement.

'You dare,' she warned him, wondering if it was really possible to be stretched like this and survive the pleasure. 'I'll take it anyway you like,' she managed shakily.

Ruiz soothed her with one hand while he increased her pleasure with the other. 'Don't be scared, I've got you,' he said, reading her.

'But it's too much,' she exclaimed frantically. 'Too big...'

'I decide when,' Ruiz told her, perfectly in control.

She trusted him and stared deep into his eyes as he

held her firmly in position to take her on an effortless slide into a world of sensation. 'I can't hold on,' she cried at last.

'You're not supposed to,' Ruiz assured her with amusement. Taking her deep with several firm, sure strokes, he thrust her over the edge where she had no option but to fall, clutching at him wildly as a starburst of sensation exploded in her head.

He held her in his arms as she slowly subsided. Holly was like an open book, pure and true, but was he ready for this wealth of feeling? He had often joked with his brothers about finding a woman who meant more to him than any other. They had tossed the idea around and concluded that as the youngest, it definitely wouldn't be Ruiz first. Probably wouldn't be him ever. Where would he find someone to put up with him? And if he did it would be years from now. He was too wild, too selfish, too unworthy of the sort of commitment and responsibility that came with devoting himself to one person, because that was what love meant to him—

*Love?*

He actually laughed out loud, and then felt guilty when Holly lifted her sated face to search his eyes. Smoothing the hair from her damp brow, he reassured her with murmured words and kisses. But she wasn't entirely convinced. 'What was that about?' she murmured groggily.

'You,' he said. 'You're lovely—I can't believe you're here with me.'

'Didn't you get that the wrong way round?' she queried sleepily.

'I got it exactly right,' he said. And she didn't deserve to be hurt.

'Lovely?' she said, wrinkling her nose. 'You really think I'm lovely?'

'Lovely and funny, and…you make me laugh,' he finished, not used to such feelings bombarding him. 'You're a lovely person, Holly.'

'Ah,' she breathed, turning her face into his chest.

Reading her insecurities, he could have kicked himself. 'Don't you dare,' he warned. Holding Holly in his arms, he realised the past haunted them both. He had worried his little sister could hear their parents fighting. And like the rest of the Acosta boys, he had struggled to understand his father's infidelities. He'd seen the hurt in his mother's eyes. He'd seen the so-called perfect family torn apart, until all that was left was a band of brothers with a sister to protect. He would never go down that road. The thought of turning out like his father was his worst nightmare. He had no intention of settling down with a woman until all the fire had left his veins and the only thing that mattered to him was holding someone's hand…

'Where are you now?' Holly murmured. 'And where are you going?' she said as he grabbed a towel from the bed and made for the door. 'I'm going to take a shower,' he said, securing the towel around his waist. His heart filled and when she smiled back at him his mind was made up.

She could use a break, Holly concluded wryly, stretching her glowing limbs contentedly. She was still in a wonderfully dreamy recovery state, and had been worrying that she might not be able to gather herself fast enough to satisfy a man like Ruiz. Keeping up with a man like that would require regular training sessions, she reflected happily. She looked up with surprise when he came back into the room, but it was only to drop a kiss on her swollen mouth. 'Where are you going now?' she demanded softly, reaching up to him.

'Goodnight, Holly…'

Smiling drowsily, she stared into the impossibly beautiful eyes, wondering if now was the moment to admit that Ruiz had exhausted her, but with a little sleep she'd be—

'Try not to oversleep,' he was telling her. 'I know you've got work tomorrow and I don't want you to be late because I kept you up half the night. Would you like me to set your alarm for you?'

She started to frown, realising that all the heat had gone from his eyes.

'I'd never forgive myself if I were the cause of putting a curb on your career,' he murmured, caressing her face.

He was talking about work now? Ice filled her veins. This wasn't good. 'There are plenty of things to worry about apart from work,' she said. 'Wasn't that what you told me?'

'So I did,' Ruiz agreed. 'And there's something else. The repairs on my town house are nearly complete so I'll be getting out of your hair soon.'

And that was good? Ruiz seemed to think so. Maybe her brain had been blown to mush by so much amazing sex, but that did not sound good to Holly.

Lifting the duvet, Ruiz pulled it up to her chin—an action that smacked more of consideration for a maiden aunt with an attack of the vapours than a crazy-for-you, I-want-to-keep-you-warm-for-the-very-few-minutes-I'm-away-from-your-side action. 'I don't want to get too comfortable,' she complained, throwing it off again. 'I might go to sleep if I do—'

'You should sleep well now, Holly.'

'Only for a few seconds.' She laughed, but something warned her to stop talking—that this was a train wreck and she was in the middle of it. Reaching up she put her hands flat against Ruiz's chest. They'd been as intimate as two people could be, but instead of feeling any response from him all she could feel was the play of muscle beneath her hands. 'Polo must be some game,' she said lamely.

'It is.'

And Ruiz had already left her, she registered.

What had she done? What had she done wrong?

She had allowed herself to want more than Ruiz was prepared to give her, Holly reasoned as he walked across the room. She wanted all of him, not just the sex. She wanted his warmth and his humour, his intelligence and perception, and the friendship that brought them close, making them, she had believed, trusting and trusted. She did not want this cold little voice inside her saying this same thing had happened to her before.

Not quite the same—

Not the same at all, Holly reassured herself. Not so many kisses and caresses, and no genuine affection of any kind. No affection at all, in fact. Her ex had been nothing like Ruiz.

'Sleep now,' Ruiz whispered from the door.

Burying her face in the pillow, she went tense all over as if that could shut out what was happening, but she only knew one way to give and that was wholeheartedly. She couldn't divide parts of herself off and hold them back. Perhaps men could do that.

Okay, she could deal with this, Holly told herself fiercely, swinging off the bed as the door closed. Chasing after Ruiz wasn't the answer. She had no one to blame but herself. Good-looking man notices plain, uncertain Holly, and bam! She's grateful. Worse. She's hungry for affection and blind to common sense—

*But Ruiz had made her feel beautiful…*

No. She had allowed Ruiz to make her feel beautiful and desired, because that was what *she* had wanted. She had bought into the fantasy while telling her readers so earnestly that casual encounters weren't cool, they were dangerous—especially for anyone with an iota of feeling inside them. Regrets? She only had to think about the letters pouring into the agony-aunt office to know that the majority of people writing those letters lived with regret. And now she was one of them. How badly had she let her readers down?

She took a shower, thinking that would help, but she was left with exactly the same absurd impression that Ruiz was special and mustn't be allowed to slip through her fingers. That he was one of a kind—one of *her* kind; the only man she would ever want and would measure every other man against—

Oh, to hell with that! Holly thought impatiently, tugging on fresh nightclothes. This wasn't love, it was lust. Those sexy eyes, that incredible body and the humorous curve of Ruiz's lips would be any woman's downfall.

No. Dropping onto the bed to stare blindly at the ceiling, she was finally prepared to admit that Holly Valiant's downfall was all her own doing and that Ruiz had merely been a willing accomplice.

*And love?*

Love didn't come into it, Holly told her inner voice coldly. Ruiz had been caught up in the moment and she had too. At least he hadn't presented her with a bill, which was pretty much what her ex had done. Shaking her head, Holly remembered that classic excuse when she had challenged her ex about emptying her bank account. 'Consider it payment for services rendered,' he'd said. 'You don't think I'd do it for free with you, do you?'

With that ringing in her ears it was no wonder she had a few issues where men were concerned—

But Ruiz wasn't that man. And she was a survivor who could put experiences like that behind her. Hadn't she already shown she could do that? Wasn't that why she was here now? She just had to get a handle on how she felt about Ruiz and remember that thunderbolts struck other people—in novels, mostly. They certainly didn't strike Holly Valiant. Tonight she had lapsed from the path she wanted to take, but she would be firmly back in control by tomorrow.

She lay in bed listening to the wind in the trees, and remained in the same lifeless position until everything in the apartment went quiet. It occurred to her that Ruiz wouldn't be lying in bed staring at the ceiling as he raked over the events of the night. This was, after all, just one day in the life of a playboy. Turning her face into the pillow, she wished briefly with amusement that she had her own agony aunt to write to and ask for advice, but then accepted she'd got it right from the start with rule number one: rely on no one but yourself.

Holly was a fixture in Ruiz's head the next morning as he pounded down the staircase to the street rather than taking the lift in the penthouse. He couldn't stop beating himself up about what had happened. She was new to London—and vulnerable. And his sister's friend. And he didn't need reminding about the world of inexperience on Holly's side and the equal amount of should-know-better on his. Exiting the building he saw his breath turn to frost. It made him long for the warmth of Argentina. Seeing Holly in Argentina away from her computer and the fantasy life she was weaving, Holly relaxed and happy, living in the real world for once… But he had meant it when he'd told Holly he would never stand in the way of her career. She had come so far since moving to London and had never made any secret of the fact that her career meant everything to her. He should be exhilarated at the thought of returning to Argentina, just as he should be happy for Holly. She was a proper city girl now—a survivor, successful and driven—

But he had hoped for more.

Ruiz frowned as he gunned the engine and pulled out onto an almost empty London street. Thank goodness today was all about business and he'd have no chance to think about Holly at all. It had to be early, he reflected wryly, for the streets of London to be this deserted. He'd lain awake after he'd left her, thinking, trying not to feel... In the end, he just left her a note warning her how cold it was and advising her to wrap up—

Holly...

He wasn't doing all that well at shutting his mind to her, Ruiz reflected. But he must. He would. He had to fly to Argentina for the match and would stay on for a while. Resting his chin on his arm as he waited for the lights to change, he remembered how Holly had felt in his arms, and her fresh, clean smell with the hint of vanilla—

Put Holly out of his mind? He might as well try to stop the breath in his chest. Nothing could steal away that look in her eyes when she gazed into his. Holly, dazzling and tender, quirky and funny, had a permanent place in his head. Holly wry, Holly angry, Holly spirited, taking him on. Holly hot as hell and sexy as sin—

Holly innocent and vulnerable.

Regrets?

She had them. And now he did too.

# CHAPTER EIGHT

*I have allowed myself to believe the playboy and I have something going on. How? Last night we got close—closer than I'm comfortable sharing in a public forum such as this.*

*Then he said his place was fixed and he'd be out of my hair shortly. Please don't pity me! I can do that for myself. And he wasn't proposing to turn the penthouse into a gilded cage where I can recline and paint my toenails until he finds time to visit, because as far as the playboy is concerned I am yesterday's news. Better to have lusted and lost than never to have lusted at all? Maybe we've all thought that at one time or another. Maybe we've all been wrong.*

*And the playboy? He's just the same—i.e. confident and busy, leaving me to get on with my life while he gets on with his. Which is ideal—or it should be, but I want someone to share things with, without getting laughed at or dismissed and he would never do that. I'd like to be part of his life—the private part that doesn't get written about—little things like sharing glances and second-guessing each other that's nothing and everything in the end. Maybe I deserve your pity after all...*

SHE had got exactly what she deserved for allowing reality and fantasy to collide, Holly concluded, impatiently dashing away tears as she walked back to the penthouse after taking Bouncer for his early morning walk. She and Ruiz might have clung to each other and gazed into each other's eyes, and in the throes of passion she might have believed anything was possible, but he was still going back to Argentina.

Leaving her to get on with her career. Wasn't that exactly what she wanted? What she should want? What it was safest to want? So, why did she feel as if the bottom had just dropped out of her world?

This was all grist to the publishing mill, Holly concluded as she opened the door on an empty apartment. She should make use of the angst and write something to entertain. No one read the 'Living with a Playboy' feature to hear her moaning. She'd make something funny out of it—

*Really?*

So the idea just hadn't come to her yet, Holly reasoned, gazing out of the window at the frigid London street with its powdering of frost. But it would, she determined, stripping off her coat. Flinging her beanie and scarf onto a chair, she tossed out her hair. Ruiz was right about it being freezing outside. But why should he care if she was well wrapped up or not? Perhaps he didn't like the idea of his dog-walker-in-chief getting sick—

Enough Ruiz.

*Enough! Enough! Out of my head now!*

There was something she wanted to do before she left for work, and it did run contrary to rule number one: rely on no one but yourself. But desperate times called for desperate measures. Most of the mail for the agony-aunt column came in anonymously—and who needed help more than she did? She hurried to her laptop and quickly created an e-mail address for this one, very special purpose, and then, typing in the message, she pressed Send before she had the chance to change her mind.

So this is what it feels like to be a dedicated career woman, Holly reflected, ready for work, having applied more make-up than usual. Were her lips supposed to feel as if they were superglued together? Grimacing as she peeled them apart, she removed the overdose of gloss with a tissue, then reclaimed her nightclothes from the floor where Ruiz had flung them the night before. Resolutely shutting her mind to thoughts of how they had come to be on the floor, she tossed them into the washing basket, but then she couldn't resist plucking out the top again on the pretext of checking if it had more than one button missing. She held it briefly to her face and inhaled, as if Ruiz's spicy scent might still linger in the brushed cotton folds.

What was she doing? She wanted no reminders of last night. Dropping the top into the basket, she picked up the cryptic note Ruiz had left her about the cold weather and aimed it at the bin. She was ready for anything now—and positively buzzing with ideas for the column. Last night was another learning experience in her new London life, and this morning was a reflection of the woman she had become, i.e. tough Holly—tougher, anyway. Holly who could handle anything, Holly who had grown up overnight and who no one would ever accuse of being naïve again.

She carried that thought to the office, where she was relieved to be rushed off her feet. It gave her no time to think—except about Ruiz, who coloured all her thoughts. They were so busy on the agony-aunt column it looked as if they might have to recruit more people to handle the level of traffic the web site was attracting, not to mention the circulation boost the magazine had received.

All thanks to your column, Holly was told to her embarrassment. 'We're a team,' she insisted as everyone from the neighbouring offices gathered round her.

'And the team loves reading about your disastrous love life,' someone commented, which made everyone else laugh.

'Who doesn't love to sit knitting at the foot of the guillotine?' another colleague added with brutal honesty and an ironic laugh.

But it was just that bad, Holly thought, wishing she could write her own happy ending. Then one of the men from marketing distracted her by brandishing a copy of the magazine. 'Your private life's not your own any more, Holly. It belongs to all of us now.'

'Great.' She forced a laugh.

'Listen up, everyone,' one of the girls announced, reading from the monitor. 'You won't believe what some idiot has written.'

Holly knew. She knew immediately and only wished she could disappear in a puff of smoke, but it was too late as her colleagues had already rounded her up and were shepherding her towards the screen.

The girl started reading Holly's message: '"I've just met a really hot guy, which is great. What's not so great is that I slept with him on practically the first night when I know the relationship isn't going anywhere. It certainly can't now as he just told me he's moving on. I know you'll say I should forget him and move on myself. And I would. I really would, but I think I've fallen for him..."' Can you believe anyone would be that stupid?' the girl demanded, directing the question at Holly.

'Don't be harsh,' Holly blurted, blushing furiously.

'No, you're right,' the girl agreed when everyone had finally calmed down and stopped laughing. 'That was bitchy of me. And we've all been there, haven't we?'

When Holly's colleagues finally calmed down and agreed with this, their team leader, who was in the best of moods for once, called for silence. 'I've got some really good news for all of us. Since the playboy told our beloved redhead Holly that they were splitting, hits to the web site are threatening to crash the system.'

'Hasn't the "Living with a Playboy" feature almost run its course?' Holly suggested desperately, not wanting to go any deeper into this. 'Should we be thinking of going out on a high? Maybe trying to come up with a new idea for a fresh column?' She was clutching at straws, Holly realised when she saw the disapproval on her team leader's face.

'Are you mad?' he demanded. 'Don't even think about finishing it. Most of the hits are on your page. Your love life is such a mess everyone feels confident writing to you.'

'Oh, good. My life is a disaster, so everyone's happy—'

'Don't be so naïve, Holly. This is fiction. Keep up the misery,' the team leader advised. 'It sells almost as well as sex.'

Everyone laughed except Holly, who had closed her mind to the problems of real life and was already constructing her next headline: *Fall in love with his dog by all means, but don't fall in love with him—especially if you expect the same level of loyalty and affection you get from his furry friend.*

When she got back to the penthouse Holly's heart almost stopped when she found Ruiz already back from work.

He was lounging on the sofa in the living room with one jean-clad leg crossed nonchalantly over the other, the sleeves rolled back on his checked shirt—

Forearms bared meant action, Holly thought, feeling a jolt as her sixth sense kicked in. Ruiz had made no secret of the fact that he would be leaving soon for the polo match in Argentina. How soon? Very soon? She could sense change in the air. And then she saw what he was looking at. 'What's this?' he demanded, swinging his laptop round so she could see the screen.

'Fiction,' she said flatly. He'd read her latest article, which was less than complimentary about him and even less kind to her. It was the type of relationship screw-up the team leader had asked for, and, because she was still stinging from Ruiz's cold dismissal and the thought of him leaving for Argentina, for once she'd given her team leader what he'd asked for—no holds barred. 'Don't you like it?' she asked Ruiz, aching inside.

'It doesn't matter what I think,' he said, closing the lid. 'It's up to your readers, though you make your feelings clear enough.'

Wait until he read tomorrow's column, Holly thought, wondering briefly if she should tone it down, and then deciding not. 'I'm a journalist, Ruiz.'

'You mean you make things up,' he said, his eyes dark and watchful.

'You know I do. I've never made any secret of the fact that the "Living with a Playboy" feature is a fiction—a piece of light entertainment to increase reader interest in the agony-aunt column.'

'A feature for which I am the inspiration.'

'I have never made a secret of that either.'

Ruiz wouldn't look at her. But he had always known what she was doing. She must appear as nonchalant as he did. The sex had been spectacular between them last night, but acting cool the morning after was the only thing she could do to protect herself. So what would she tell her readers? She would heap on the misery as she'd been asked to, Holly concluded. 'What's wrong, Ruiz?'

'You say this is fiction?' He glanced at the laptop. 'But I think this must reflect your true feelings, at least a little.' And as such it hurt like hell, Ruiz concluded angrily. On the back of it he'd made a lot of changes—like hiring a housekeeper to take care of Bouncer while he was gone. 'I think you've started believing your own fiction, Holly.'

'What?' She laughed incredulously. 'It's just work. That's what I do.'

'Then I don't like what you do.'

The room hung in frigid silence. Holly felt as if the sword of Damocles were hanging by a thread above her head. She knew the sword had to fall, it was just a question of when and how fast.

*So get out of its way—*

'I'll go and put these things away, if you don't mind?' she said, glancing at the shopping bags of food she had brought in.

'When you've done that, come back. We need to talk.'

She felt dead inside. There was nothing in Ruiz's voice to suggest that last night had meant anything to him. Just as she had suspected, he had already moved on.

She went into the kitchen, where Bouncer came snuffling up to her, his big brown eyes soulful as if the dog sensed her tension and wanted to defuse it. 'I won't leave you,' Holly vowed fiercely. 'I'll find somewhere to live where you can come with me.' She glanced at the door behind which the man she had been so confident she could turn into a fiction, and who had somehow become so much more than that, was waiting for her.

She'd miss him when he left.

Squeezing back tears, she made do with hugging Ruiz's dog. 'I love you, Bouncer,' she said passionately, releasing some of the tension. It wasn't right to feel like this about a man. No excuses. She'd known all along how dangerous it was to risk her heart.

'I thought you were going to put that shopping away and then come back and talk?'

Collecting herself quickly, Holly looked up to find Ruiz lounging in the doorway. His arms were folded across his formidable chest, and his voice, his body, his eyes especially—eyes she had stared into with love, and into which she had placed her trust—everything drew her to him. She couldn't change her feelings where Ruiz was concerned just because it was safer to do so or because she willed it. She could write whatever she liked in the column, but reality refused to be manipulated. 'I'm just sorting stuff out,' she managed casually.

'Well, don't take all evening.'

The playboy might be a fictional figure, but Ruiz was all too real. And so were her feelings for him. Finding the doggy treats she'd bought at the supermarket, she tried telling herself it wasn't all bad as Bouncer's tail thanked her profusely. At least she'd made one good friend in London. But there was really only one friend and lover she could ever want, and he plainly wasn't interested.

She took her time, had a shower and changed into jeans before returning to the living room where Ruiz was working on his laptop. 'You're leaving soon, aren't you?' She had to challenge him before he could make the announcement. Ruiz's answer was to indicate the space next to him on the sofa. She sat as far away from him as she could, determined not to let him see how she felt about his silence. She wondered then if Ruiz had any lingering memories of her touch, or her kisses, as she had of his. Did men even bank physical memories like a woman, to pull out and review later?

She had to stop thinking like that, or she'd break down. She should have had a good howl in the shower to get this out of her system. The way Ruiz was acting, so casual and normal as if this was just another day, she couldn't bear it. The greatest intimacy of all seemed to have pushed them apart, and she of all people should have known the risks: *don't tie me down, don't ask me to commit.* It was, after all, a favourite topic in the column. Friends were bound by loving ties even if they didn't see each other for years, but sleep with a friend and that changed everything, because you ran the risk of becoming a nuisance, a potential curb on your friend's freedom.

'Are you okay?' Ruiz glanced at her with concern as she sucked in a couple of steadying breaths.

'I'm fine, thank you. So when are you going?'

'Soon. Very soon. But that's not what I want to talk to you about.' He picked up a set of keys. Was Ruiz offering Holly the keys to his house? Why? 'Do you want me to keep an eye on the place while you're away?' She was happy to do so.

'No, that's okay—but thanks for the offer. I have employed a live-in housekeeper who will have her own apartment on site.' He ruffled Bouncer's ears. Having padded into the room in search of company, the big dog had settled down between them. 'The town house is a much better option than here,' Ruiz went on. 'There's a proper garden, plus a large communal garden that leads on to the park.'

'That's great.' She kept it light. 'But I'm not sure I can afford the rent...'

'That's very funny,' Ruiz said, shaking his head, but his eyes were cold as he stared at her. 'I'm talking about Bouncer moving back there. You'll stay here, won't you, Holly? At least until you find somewhere else to live. No hurry,' he stressed.

'Of course.' She laughed. She smiled. She died a little more inside. She should have known Ruiz's forward planning was all about his dog. 'Don't worry, I won't be here long. I've found several flats to look at in the next couple of days—'

'Well, that's great,' Ruiz agreed. 'But you know you can stay on here as long as you want.'

'I'd rather not.'

'Okay.' He shrugged. 'Whatever you want, Holly...'

'I thought I'd move closer to the office.'

Ruiz made no comment and it was a relief to get up and turn away. New Holly didn't long for things she couldn't have. She didn't risk her heart or her bank account. And she certainly didn't risk her career, Holly told herself fiercely, fighting back tears.

# CHAPTER NINE

*Concerned you might be left on the shelf? Don't be. Just think—no shirts to iron, no meals to cook, and you can eat chocolate éclairs for supper every night of your life.*

*Light-bulb moment, why? Because wallowing in misery isn't for me, the new me. Friend to lover and back to friends again. I'm told this shift of position is possible if handled correctly. And because I love this man's sister as if she were my own and I don't want to hurt her, I'm determined to make it back to friends with him.*

*And the playboy? Who knows what he thinks? He's off to Argentina and a life of which I will never be a part. I have to say he seems preoccupied. Perhaps he's concerned he's been out of the game too long and might not come up to scratch when he returns to play top class polo. Whatever his problem, one thing I'm sure about—it has nothing to do with me.*

HOLLY kept her head down next day at the office. Work was the only thing that numbed the pain of thinking about Ruiz resuming the life of a playboy in the next couple of days, surrounded by sloe-eyed *señoritas* in

Argentina. Work, as well as time-tabling visits to likely rental properties throughout the capital…

'You haven't forgotten it's the Christmas party to-night, have you?' Freya reminded Holly later that same afternoon.

'Hmm?' Holly barely looked up as she hammered away on her keyboard.

'Didn't you hear me?' Freya pressed.

'I heard you, but I have to work.'

'For goodness' sake, Holly. You haven't even stopped for lunch,' Freya protested.

'We're not letting you get out of it,' several more girls chorused as they gathered round Holly's desk.

'You haven't forgotten the Christmas party is at the samba club, have you?' Freya prompted, exchanging glances with her friends.

How could she forget? Another good reason for not going to the party, Holly reasoned, thinking of Ruiz and keeping her head down when the girls shrieked *'Ole!'* while putting in a bit of skirt-twirling and pouting prac-tice.

'Hot men, fast music, free drinks. How can you pass that up?' Freya demanded.

'Easily,' Holly murmured, keeping her attention fixed on the screen.

'Well, we're not going without you,' Freya said flatly.

'Then none of us will go,' Holly flashed, immediately regretting her outburst when she saw the hurt and sur-prise on Freya's face. But how could she go to the samba club with all that it meant to her? It had been such a spe-cial night with Ruiz—a night she would never be able to recreate or forget, and she didn't want to try. 'Please, Freya. I've still got so much to do,' she pleaded, offering her last piece of chocolate, which Freya refused. 'Some other night, perhaps.'

'Holly, this is the Christmas party,' Freya pointed out. 'It won't come around again until next year. You never stop working. You're in serious danger of—'

'Don't say becoming boring. Please don't say that,' Holly cut in.

'I was about to say, you're in danger of burning out,' Freya told her with concern.

'I'm sorry,' Holly admitted. 'Truly, I am.' And when Freya smiled encouragement, she added in a very different voice, 'Okay, so whose bright idea was it to hold the Christmas party at the samba club?'

Freya's face brightened immediately. 'The guys in marketing. Does that mean you're coming?'

'If you'll have me,' Holly said wryly.

Freya's answer was to switch off her screen. 'Go and get ready,' she insisted. 'We'll wait for you.'

She had made some good friends in London, Holly reflected as the girls bustled her out of the office. She should make more time for them, but somehow there didn't seem to be time for anything these days.

Having tested every part of his body at the gym and found it all in good working order, Ruiz took a long, cold shower and tucked a towel around his waist. He was just opening his locker when the call came through on his phone. 'Gabe? To what do I owe this honour?'

'That pretty little thing you brought to the club that time?'

'Do you mean Holly?' Ruiz was instantly alert, all thoughts of cutting Holly out of his life forgotten.

'*ROCK!* is having its Christmas party at the club and the guys are well into the party spirit. I'm not sure your friend is too happy about them trying to get her to dance. Would you like me to intervene?'

A muscle in Ruiz's jaw flexed. 'I'm only across the road at the gym. Can you keep an eye on things until I get there?'

'Count on it.'

He didn't pause to dry his hair. Throwing on the same running clothes he had arrived in, he collected Bouncer from the girls on Reception and headed off.

How was she going to do this nicely without causing offence to people she had to work with? How was she going to get out of dancing with men who'd had too much to drink, and who should have learned by now that no meant no? She couldn't help but remember Ruiz, and how safe she'd felt with him.

'Ow! You're hurting me,' Holly protested, freeing her arm from one man's grasp. 'Please don't touch me,' she exclaimed, whirling round to try and catch another culprit. But the more Holly resisted, the more the men seemed to think it was a game. Where was Freya? Where were all the other girls she worked with? Holly frantically scanned the dance floor, but it was so packed she couldn't see anyone she knew.

And then her heart rolled over. 'Ruiz?'

Dressed in running shoes and gym clothes, his hair still damp from the shower, Ruiz was framed in the entrance to the club with Bouncer sitting patiently at his feet. With his dark eyes narrowed Ruiz was also searching the dance floor, every fibre of his pumped and muscular body poised for action. The moment he caught sight of her he strode purposefully forward. A path cleared in front of him. No wonder, Holly thought. The expression in Ruiz's eyes was murderous. With their reflexes dulled by drink, the men around her took a little longer to realise what was happening, but thankfully some primal warning mechanism must have kicked in and they peeled away just in time.

'Are you all right?' Ruiz demanded tersely.

She was now, Holly realised, feeling massive relief.

'I heard you were having trouble.' Before she could question this, Ruiz added, 'Let's get your coat.' And putting a protective arm around her shoulders, he led her towards the reception area.

'You've come straight from the gym,' she said as they collected Bouncer.

'No, I always dress like this for a night out.'

'Ruiz, I—'

'Don't say it.'

'I will say it. I always seem to be such a bother. So, thank you.'

Ruiz grunted and held the door for her.

They walked home at a brisk pace through the park, icy air billowing in silent clouds from their mouths. They both had plenty to think about, but neither of them voiced those thoughts, and Holly could feel Ruiz's tension. Only Bouncer seemed perfectly at ease as he trotted along between them. She was grateful to the big dog's softening influence on a situation that showed no sign of easing any time soon. Ruiz didn't speak until they reached the penthouse and then he turned at the door of the elevator. 'What will you do when I'm not here, Holly?'

'Work,' she said as the doors slid open and they stepped inside.

Ruiz firmed his jaw, staring straight ahead as they waited for the elevator to reach the penthouse floor. While she knew she had done nothing wrong Holly felt as if something light and good had died inside her and she didn't know how to get it back. 'I suppose you can forgive the people at the Christmas party. Thank goodness it only comes round once a year.'

Ruiz remained resolutely unimpressed by her attempt to make light of something that could so easily have turned nasty without his intervention. When the lift doors opened he stood aside to let her pass. She wasn't even sure he was going to get out with her. 'Thank you for coming to the club. I don't know what I'd have done if you hadn't been there.'

He indicated that she should move and he would follow. 'If you will excuse me, Holly,' Ruiz said, holding the door for her, 'I'm going back home to bed.'

'You're taking Bouncer? Of course you are,' she said quickly, remembering Bouncer was living at the town house now. 'I'm really sorry to have put you to all this trouble, Ruiz. The silly thing is I didn't even want to go out. I'm so bogged down with work I can't spare the time.' She stopped when she saw his expression.

'I think you have some decisions to make about how you live your life, Holly. Success is great, but—'

Ruiz's shrug said it all.

'I need to get some sleep,' he said, turning. Before he made the long journey back to Argentina, Holly guessed, as the man she loved and his dog left her life without a backward glance.

He didn't sleep. Luckily for him he'd packed for the trip ahead of time. He tossed and turned, thinking about life and what he wanted out of it, and he came up with the same answer every time: Holly. She was all he wanted. He couldn't make sense of his longing for her, or come up with anything more concrete than the fact that his life was empty without her. He wanted her, not just for a fling, but for longer—for ever, maybe. He'd started to get to know her and he wanted to know more. A lot more. He wanted to give them a chance. He wanted to run with the crazy redhead and see where it led. Almost certainly nowhere, Ruiz concluded, since Holly seemed completely wrapped up in her career. But was that because she really didn't care about anything apart from her job. Or did Holly's lack of confidence in her personal life mean she only felt safe when living vicariously through her column? There was only one way to find out.

If the team leader wanted misery he could have it, Holly reflected the next morning as she hung up her coat at the office. The only consolation was that she wasn't alone with her hangdog expression. Everyone was a little under par after the party, moving in slow-mo and speaking in mumbles, and then only when necessary. But all that changed when she reached her desk. 'What?' she said, looking at the mob surrounding it. 'What's happened?'

As her colleagues peeled away from Holly's work station Holly saw the envelope propped against the monitor. She knew immediately who it was from. Thousands of letters arrived each week addressed to The Redhead, but this was addressed in bold, black script, To Holly.

'Well? Open it,' Freya insisted.

Picking it up, Holly held the envelope to her chest almost as if she hoped that would make it invisible. 'This is private,' she said, hoping everyone would go away.

'Open it here,' Holly's team leader insisted with his usual insensitivity. 'Then if it's anything to upset you, one of us can take over your work so at least something will get done today.'

'He's all heart,' one of the girls murmured discreetly, adding, 'We're all on your side, Holly. And judging by the size of that envelope there could be something more inside it than just a private note.'

And why should she care if it was from Ruiz? Holly reasoned. He'd made it clear enough last night that what he wanted was a clean break. Perhaps she'd left something behind in the club and he was returning it, though she couldn't remembering doing so—

'It's a folder from an airline,' Freya informed her colleagues as Holly peered inside the envelope. 'And there's something else,' she exclaimed, poring over Holly's shoulder.

'Do you mind?' Holly said shakily. Walking over to the window, she turned her back on everyone. She read the handwritten note first. It was another of Ruiz's succinct wake-up-calls: 'Have you thought about your life yet, Holly? About who you really want to be? Maybe the enclosed will help. Ruiz.'

'Are you okay, Holly?' Freya demanded when she remained rooted to the spot. 'Have you checked the airline tickets yet?'

Airline tickets, Holly thought numbly, turning her attention to the rest of the envelope's contents. 'Oh, my God! This is ridiculous—'

'What is?' Holly's team leader demanded.

'First-class return tickets to Buenos Aires, leaving tonight. And a VIP pass to a polo match.' Holly held them up as if she needed everyone else to confirm that they were real. When the shrieks of excitement died down, she shook her head. 'What a waste.'

'A waste?' her team leader queried sharply.

'Well, I won't be using them.' Going back to her desk, Holly sank weakly into her chair. 'How can I, when I've got so much work on here?'

'Have laptop, will travel,' the team leader argued

briskly, swinging his chair round. 'You can send copy from anywhere in the world with Internet access, Holly. And if you don't take up that offer, you can consider yourself fired.'

'Fired?' Holly exclaimed, springing up.

'Wasn't it you who told me that the "Living with a Playboy" feature had almost run its course?' her boss reminded her. 'Don't you think this trip to Argentina is the key to reviving it?'

And put her life through the wringer again? Did she want that? Wouldn't it be so much easier to make it all up in the column as she went along and walk away from this? 'I can't afford to take time off,' she said flatly.

'We'll cover your expenses and pay your wages while you're away, as long as you keep submitting the column,' the team leader said, growing in enthusiasm as he thought through his idea. 'You've just been appointed *ROCK!*'s foreign correspondent. Just think what that will do for reader figures,' he added, rubbing his hands with glee.

Reader figures. Great. But she felt empty inside. What was wrong with her? She finally had the career she'd always wanted.

And what a hollow victory that had turned out to be. What about the guy? What about Ruiz?

The thought of seeing Ruiz again was a terrifying and uncertain prospect. She didn't know what to expect. Could she do it? Could she be with Ruiz again, write about him, and remain aloof? 'What about me?' she blurted as desperation took over.

'What about you?' the team leader demanded. 'You're part of a team, Holly. The clue's in the word.'

He was right, Holly realised. She couldn't let the team down—all of their jobs were on the line, not just hers.

And nothing was ever achieved by hiding away. She had to get out there and confront life—and Ruiz—head-on.

'I don't know what you're standing there for,' he added impatiently. 'Shouldn't you be going back home to pack? According to this ticket you've got four hours to catch your flight!'

# CHAPTER TEN

*Hope I can read my writing later with all the turbulence—this must be the messiest diary entry I've made in a while.*

*Did I have any option but to accept Ruiz's invitation? Having already messed up my non-existent love life, can I afford to risk my job as well? And then I have to ask myself this: If I can't trust myself to take a professional approach and write an article about the playboy without wailing, what kind of journalist am I going to make?*

*So here I am after a thirteen hour flight, taxiing towards the stand at Aeropuerto Ministro Pistarini airport, more commonly known as Ezeiza after the city close to Buenos Aires in which the airport is situated. Did you hear that? Buenos Aires! Where the weather, according to our hip young captain, is a bikini-basting twenty-eight degrees. Before you get excited, he wasn't directing that comment at me. With my red hair and freckles I don't feel a bit out of place amongst all the sultry whip-thin señoritas seated here with me in First Class. As if! I feel more like a suet dumpling than ever—a fact no doubt observed by said captain when he took the precaution of performing a talent-trawl in the*

*First Class cabin before lowering his landing gear.
But I will be spending Christmas with the playboy
at his family's fabulous country-sized estancia and
no one else can say that. I think you'll agree this
takes 'Living with a Playboy' to a whole new level.
Buckle your seat belts, my friends; something tells
me we're in for a bumpy ride.*

THE first thing Holly saw in the terminal building was
a huge poster advertising the polo match featuring the
Band of Brothers. Ruiz Acosta, ten times life size and
easily the best looking of four astonishingly handsome
brothers, staring down at her. She swallowed deeply.
Everywhere she looked there seemed to be another
poster—another heart-stopping reminder of the darkly
glittering glamour that had so easily attracted her. Even
the limousine Ruiz had sent to collect her had a Band of
Brothers sticker on the back window. A crowd had gathered round to stare and comment and swoon, and by the
time she had collapsed onto the back seat her heart was
thundering like a pack of wild mustangs.

Surely, this had to be a dream…

But it wasn't a dream, and as the luxury vehicle ate
up the dusty miles between the airport and the Acosta
family's *estancia* Holly felt her throat grow increasingly
tight. Her anxiety wasn't eased by the sight of numerous
billboards advertising the match. Ruiz was a national
hero it seemed. But how could this swarthy, dangerous-
looking man with his burning stare, earring and tattoos
be the same man who had held her in his arms and made
love to her—

Forget that. Forget him. You're here to do your job,
that's it.

She couldn't think of anything but Ruiz. Even this

harsh land was right for him. London, with all its neatly packaged districts, felt a lifetime away as the driver took her deeper into the interior. She had been commissioned to write an article and nothing more, Holly reasoned, trying to calm down: 'Christmas with the Playboy'. She would also have the chance to watch Ruiz play polo, to see this rugged man with his thighs wrapped around the flanks of some prime horseflesh.

'The game will have started by the time we arrive,' the driver informed her. 'But you'll see plenty of it,' he assured her in heavily accented English. 'That's if there's anyone left alive on the field for you to watch by the time we get there.'

He laughed. She didn't laugh.

Another colossal billboard loomed in front of them like a vivid punctuation mark amidst miles of arid scrubland that seemed to mock her with just how far she was from civilisation and any form of escape. She stared blindly out of the window. What was she doing here? Why had she come? She could have refused.

She should have refused.

*And lost her job?*

A road that had been deserted for hours was suddenly clogged with vehicles all travelling in the same direction. Hundreds more were already parked up on the roadside and in lines across the fields. Holly gasped with alarm when her driver, using the simple avoidance tactic of pulling onto the wrong side of the road, overtook everything at speed. With a final thump on his horn to warn the other vehicles, he swung the wheel and steered the limousine beneath an impressive archway that led to an immaculately groomed drive lined with trees. 'Welcome to Estancia Acosta, Señorita Valiant,' he said, continuing to drive at a speed that had the crowds spraying to either side on the road ahead of them. 'I'm going to take you straight round to the pony lines where you will find Ruiz, if he isn't on the polo field.'

'I'll be fine here. You can drop me anywhere.' But preferably not beneath this billboard, Holly thought anxiously as they drove through what looked more like a very busy small town than a family ranch.

'You might get lost if I leave you here,' the driver insisted. 'And then I'd be in trouble.'

With whom? she wondered. With Ruiz?

'My orders are quite specific,' the driver went on. 'This is the most popular event of the year.'

It looked like it, and she was thrilled to see real gauchos, the Argentine equivalent of a cowboy, for the first time. Leather chaps to protect their breeches were held up by coin-decorated belts, while their hats were festooned with bands and laces. There were socialites too—the girls as immaculately groomed as the flashy polo ponies they had come to see. While I am more your sturdy hunter, Holly thought wryly. But then she was hunting for a story, not a husband.

But that didn't stop her finger-combing her hair as the driver started to slow the car. They were approaching the pony lines now. Mashing her lips together, she decided against lipstick because her hands were shaking too much to put it on. She couldn't see the polo field as it was hidden by the towering stands, but polo players were stalking about like muscular gods of the game. They wore white, jean-style breeches and either black shirts with a skull and cross-bones embroidered on the pocket, or 'Acosta' emblazoned in white in capital letters on the back of red shirts. Some of the players were already mounted with their faceguards down, their dark eyes shielded behind stylish eye-protectors, but so far there was no sign of Ruiz.

'He must be playing,' the driver said as a cheer went up somewhere out of sight. 'These men are the reserves—warming up and standing ready in case of injury.'

Holly's stomach lurched at the thought of Ruiz being injured.

'Shall I take you to see him play?'

'Would you?' she said gratefully, though the thought terrified her at the same time.

The stands were vast and impressive and ran the length of the field, which was about six times the size of a football pitch and packed to the rafters with noisy supporters. Seats had been reserved for them on the front row and as she sat down Holly's gaze instantly locked onto Ruiz. She'd have known that muscular body any-where, though she had never seen it at full stretch like this. As he thundered past the stand in a blur of red top, and white mud-streaked breeches, she felt a reckless punch of full-blown lust. Ruiz's face guard was down, but she didn't need to see his eyes to know that he was on a mission and everyone had better keep out of his way. The romantic idea of polo was one thing, but see-ing Ruiz's superb horsemanship firsthand, along with his tactical expertise and sheer physical courage, made it impossible to keep her thoughts confined to business. She was ashamed to admit, even to herself, how much she wanted him.

No, she didn't, Holly told herself firmly, turning like the rest of the crowd to watch Ruiz. She wasn't going there. She was a professional journalist with a job to do. Ruiz had stopped abruptly at one end of the field. Turning his horse, he charged the pack at a gallop, mal-let raised. Leaning at such an acute angle, he seemed to defy gravity as he deftly hooked the ball and smacked it down the field. The crowd went wild as the band of brothers closed ranks behind him. Everyone sprang to their feet, screaming encouragement as Ruiz swung his mallet a second time and scored a goal. Forgetting herself, Holly screamed hysterically with the rest.

'What a man,' the woman next to her exclaimed, fanning herself with her hand. 'What wouldn't I give to spend the night with him?'

So that was why she had come to Argentina, Holly thought wryly.

*No, it wasn't!*

'Ruiz stole that ball from the great Nero Caracas,' the driver on her other side was explaining to her excitedly. 'Ruiz's brother Nacho Acosta and Nero Caracas are considered to be the top players in the world.'

'And yet Ruiz got the better of him,' Holly agreed with pride. Oh, yes, he did.

She watched Ruiz settle back into the saddle and take easy control of his horse as the two teams cantered down the field to change ends after his goal. He was so relaxed, so sexy. The excitement of the match had made her forget how nervous she had been at the prospect of seeing him again, but now the butterflies were back. What would a man like that think of a distinctly unglamorous, plane-rumpled Holly Valiant? Would he sigh heavily, and wonder why on earth she had agreed to come to Argentina? Ruiz must know why she had accepted. The public reason was that she had no option if she didn't want to lose her job. The private reason was hers alone.

She sat tensely as the match started up again. The camaraderie between Ruiz and his infamous brothers was obvious, as was the strong bond between them. The way he praised his horse touched her, just as the quiet confidence on his ruthless face made Ruiz even more attractive. She envied him for belonging so strongly to something and somewhere, and having the family bond she had always hankered after. How wonderful for Lucia to have grown up under the protection of brothers like that, she thought briefly, but then she added wryly, how terrible. With four warriors watching over her it was no wonder Lucia Acosta had felt the need to break away. The Acosta brothers were such a formidable force it would be easy to be eclipsed by them.

When the match had been declared a draw and the players awarded their medals, they cantered off the field. Holly felt weak with longing, and tense with anticipation at the thought of this first meeting. She left her seat to go and find Ruiz. The teams were coming into the yard by the time she arrived, steel horseshoes clattering across the cobbles. The men made quite a sight—all of them muscular and rugged, with shoulders wide enough to carry an ox. She stood beneath the shade of some trees, watching discreetly as the men chatted to each other as if they hadn't been mortal enemies only minutes before. Ruiz had his mallet resting on his massive shoulders, and was holding the reins casually in one hand. He was so achingly familiar, and yet a stranger in so many ways. Thinking herself hidden in the shadows she exclaimed out loud when he looked straight at her and came cantering over.

'Welcome to Argentina, Holly Valiant,' he said.

She gasped with surprise when he dipped out of the saddle to kiss her cheek. 'I'm glad you decided to accept my invitation,' he said, staring down at her with all the knowledge and humour in his eyes she remembered.

She hoped she mumbled something vaguely polite in return as Ruiz sprang down from the saddle. Handing over his sweating pony and mallet to a waiting groom, he turned to face her. 'Did you enjoy the match?' Her heart thundered in response as Ruiz removed his helmet and ran one hand through his wild black hair.

'It was fantastic. You were fantastic...' Her voice tailed away. She felt incredibly self-conscious all of a sudden, and realised that Ruiz must receive such unsophisticated compliments all the time.

'I'm glad you enjoyed it,' he said, a sincere smile planting an attractive crease in his cheek. 'Did you see my goal?'

'Yes, I saw it,' she confirmed, realising that even national heroes needed reassurance from time to time. 'It was brilliant.' And now she was smiling. How could she not smile when Ruiz was around? She had lost the art of playing it cool where Ruiz Acosta was concerned—if she had ever had it in the first place.

Ruiz's massive shoulders eased in a self-deprecating shrug as he glanced after his horse. 'I owe it all to my pony. I saved my best horse until the last chukka.'

'I think it might have something to do with your skill too,' she suggested dryly, growing in confidence because Ruiz was so relaxed.

Her heart bounced as he stared intently at her. 'Are you attempting to flatter me, Señorita Valiant?'

'Maybe, Señor Acosta,' she agreed. To have Ruiz teasing her again in that warm, husky voice was alarming and yet strangely reassuring too. It was as though nothing had changed between them, as though they were still close, and had always been close, and only she had imagined the yawning gulf growing between them.

'Come on,' he said, taking hold of her arm.

'Where are you taking me?'

'Does it matter?'

Ruiz's gaze was dark and disturbing, and she had to

remind herself that this was a research trip. 'Not one bit,' she said. 'Your driver told me you and your brothers own some of the top ponies in the world...' Not the best conversational opening gambit she had ever come up with, but she had to try something to distract her wandering and highly erotic thoughts.

'Have you ever wondered why there isn't a polo world series?' Ruiz demanded, staring down at her.

She looked into the dark, compelling gaze. 'I'm sure you're going to tell me.'

'Argentina would clean up every time. We have the best ponies in the world. And the best players.'

'The most modest too,' Holly observed dryly.

'You're right,' Ruiz agreed, his eyes dancing with shared laughter. 'We're just about perfect.'

She hadn't imagined it would be so easy to relax with him. But she mustn't read too much into it, Holly warned herself. Tensions had never existed between them for long and she was Ruiz's guest in Argentina.

'I notice you're not taking notes?' Ruiz observed, adopting an expression that made her smile even more.

'What notes?' she said, frowning. And then she laughed again, knowing her reputation for work.

'I was led to understand that the only reason you agreed to accept my invitation to come to Argentina was because your boss at *ROCK!* told you it would be a good idea to write a polo feature for the magazine.'

'Correct,' she said. That was the only reason.

'And there was no other reason?' Ruiz probed in his deep, husky voice.

'Should there be?' If she couldn't fool herself, what hope was there of fooling Ruiz?

'You tell me,' he said.

* * *

'This is my family home,' Ruiz told her as they approached a grand old house.

The building had an air of permanence and was much loved, Holly decided, noticing it was immaculately maintained. When they went through the impressive entrance she found herself in a large hall crammed with people. 'Too many people for proper introductions,' Ruiz determined, leading her towards an impressive sweeping staircase. 'You should have some privacy now so you can rest up and take a bath before you meet everyone. You might even like a sleep to recover from the journey?'

'I'll be fine. I'm far too excited,' Holly admitted, which drew a sharp glance from Ruiz. 'If you can just give me half an hour or so to take a shower and change my clothes…?'

'But no face masks,' he said dryly.

'Promise,' she said, trying hard to curb a smile.

'I need to freshen up too,' Ruiz pointed out, breaking what had turned into a long moment of mutual inspection and assessment. 'Then I'm going to take a tour of the stables to check on the ponies.'

'Can I come with you?'

'If you promise not to bring your phone or your notepad.'

'I haven't even switched it on yet.' And only now remembered her oversight.

'Then do so,' Ruiz prompted. 'You should let people know you're safe. Though your working hours at the *estancia* will be between one and four in the afternoon while I'm taking a siesta.'

She laughed. 'So I work while you rest?'

'Sounds good to me,' Ruiz observed with another heart-stopping flash of humour.

'And what am I supposed to do for the rest of the time?'

'Live a little?' Ruiz suggested.

I will, she thought as he turned to go.

She had so much research material already and she'd only been here five minutes, Holly reflected as she leaned back against the heavy wooden door in her bedroom. Decorated in shades of palest coral and cream the room Ruiz had chosen for her was light and sunny, and beautifully feminine in a way Holly had never had the luxury of enjoying before. There was lace on the bed and silver on the dressing table, with a clutch of satin cushions on the elegant chaise longue positioned to take in the view over the ponies in the paddocks beyond the formal gardens.

The scent of beeswax tickled her senses as she waited for the data to upload on her phone. It was then that she noticed the family photographs arranged on the antique chest of drawers. There was a shot of the brothers as teenagers with their much younger sister, all of them smiling and instantly recognisable—dangerously handsome even then. She might only have been here five minutes, Holly reflected as her heartbeat increased, but it was long enough to know she would write about sexy polo players in general, because some things were better kept private. She couldn't bear the thought of everyone laughing at her if she admitted how hopelessly in love she was with one polo player in particular.

Having made the necessary calls, she took a shower in the old fashioned, but immaculate and beautifully maintained bathroom, before sorting out her clothes on top of the high, intricately carved four-poster bed with its dressing of crisp white linen and lace. When she was ready she went to find Ruiz and her heart juddered when she bumped into him on the landing. Like her, he was just going downstairs. 'Do you have everything you need?' he asked.

She looked at him and thought not. 'My room is lovely. Thank you.' And then the question uppermost in her mind had to be asked. 'Why did you invite me here, Ruiz?' It was impossible to tell what he was thinking.

The dark eyes gave nothing away. 'Your editor's pleased you're here, isn't he?'

'Yes, of course he is.' But that didn't answer her question and Holly's shoulders slumped as she watched Ruiz walk ahead of her down the stairs. Her heart yearned for him, but her head said, Don't set yourself up for another disaster.

## CHAPTER ELEVEN

*Another column I only hope makes more sense to you, the reader, than it does to me right now. My head is full of one man: the playboy. He's so hot and sexy with a torso that would eclipse the centre-fold on any magazine you care to mention. To see him control a horse, effortlessly and completely, is the biggest turn-on of all. The polo match was spectacular. He was spectacular—*

*Am I getting a little selfish here? If I am, this is for you: the quotient of thighs like smooth, muscular tree trunks, and forearms like hairy steel bars was totally off the scale—*

*But the playboy is the only man I'm interested in. To seem him in full battle mode cracking the ball down the field at a gallop was so thrilling I would have fallen in love with him on the spot if I weren't in love with him already.*

*Yes. You can safely say I am a lost cause. I don't seem to have any sense of reality when it comes to men. I can't find a safe man with carpet slippers and a newspaper. I can't even find a slightly risky man with a set of golf clubs and a year's subscription to the local squash club. All I can find is a Playboy with a capital P and a stonking great mallet.*

Ruiz was in the kitchen drinking coffee, with a house-keeper bustling at the stove. He put his cup down when Holly came into the room and got up immediately. 'I want you to see something,' he said, leading her back towards the door she had just entered.

His touch on her arm was so familiar...so achingly familiar. She liked it. A great deal too much.

Ruiz took her across the baronial hall with its burnished wooded floor and muted, jewel-coloured hangings to another passageway leading off the grand entrance hall. Opening the door onto a room with a very different personality, he followed her in. Leaning back against the door, he said, 'Well? What do you think?'

She was finding it hard to concentrate right now.

'Take a look around,' he said. 'I think you'll find everything you need here...'

It was an office, she realised. Ruiz had brought her into a very modern office. All teak and cream furnishings, and sunlight slid through crisp white blinds to create the perfect working environment.

'I thought you would appreciate having a room of your own to work in quietly,' he said. 'Somewhere away from the rest of the house and the hubbub of polo and family life. This is where I come when I want to get away, and where I do some of my best thinking. Let's hope the same vibes work for you. Consider this your room for the duration of your stay, Holly. No one will disturb you here.'

It was a beautiful room. So why did she feel so flat? Maybe because Ruiz wasn't part of the package? 'Thank you.' No one had ever been so thoughtful before. Her family home had been small and cramped with parents at war, so the local library or the coffee shop down the road had been her office. A room of her own, even for her brief stay here, was luxury indeed. There was only one thing missing, Holly realised as Ruiz turned to go.

'Don't spend all your time in here,' was his parting shot.

'I won't.' She was determined to keep it light. 'I won't have anything to write about if I do!'

But he'd already gone. The door had shut behind Ruiz, leaving Holly to her own devices in his fabulous office. Great. She was here to work, so this was brilliant.

Well, get on with it, then...

Nothing. Her mind was empty. There wasn't a single idea in her head. There was just a keyboard, a blank screen, and the sound of confident footsteps walking away.

There were times when you had to cast your net into the water rather than wait on the bank doing nothing, Holly reflected when the longest ten minutes of her life had passed. There was everything here in this office, except for the one thing she needed. Picking up the internal phone, she dialled the kitchen. Ruiz picked up immediately. 'Problem?' he demanded.

'I need something to write about.'

'I'll be right up.'

There was nothing in his tone to suggest that this was going to be anything more than a courtesy call, but Holly's heart turned over at the sound of a knock on the door. 'Well?' Ruiz demanded, walking in.

Her brain seized up. Right now she just wanted to look at him. There'd been a Ruiz-drought in her life and now she just wanted to drink him in. Big, refreshing gulps! Propping one lean thigh against the desk, he stared down at her, frowning. 'I hope you haven't brought me up here for nothing?'

'No...' Her senses were full of him. She loved it when he glowered, and Ruiz was close enough for her to feel the warmth of his body and smell the soap he'd used in the shower.

'Why aren't you working?' he asked, straightening up.

'I am,' she protested.

'Well, work faster,' Ruiz prompted, 'and remember that when you leave this room your work stays here. Agreed?'

She loved it when his lips firmed. 'Agreed,' she said faintly.

'Louder, Holly.'

'Agreed.'

'That's better,' Ruiz murmured. 'Now come here. We haven't said hello to each other properly yet.'

She stood. Taking a couple of small, prudent paces forward, she stretched out her hand to shake his.

Ruiz took hold of her and dragged her close. 'Hello, Holly,' he murmured, laughing down into her eyes.

She stared into the dark, amused eyes, and then at the firm, sexy mouth only a whisper from hers. 'I thought you said this room was to work in,' she protested without much force.

'It is,' Ruiz agreed. 'Here's your next headline.'

His kiss took her breath away. It was both fierce and tender. Two dams had burst at once, she thought as Ruiz swung her into his arms. 'You can't do this in the office.'

Shh you crazy woman, and savour the moment!

'I can do anything I want, anywhere I want,' Ruiz assured her. 'Just so long as you want it too...'

'All I want is you,' she said softly, opening her heart when caution couldn't save it.

'If you're sure?' He held her above the sofa. 'I can always leave you here to work.'

'You dare,' she said, feeling excitement spring inside her. 'And you know what they say about too much work.'

'I know what I say,' Ruiz commented under his breath.

'Where are we going?' she said as he carried her towards the door.

'To bed,' Ruiz said bluntly. 'This might take some time and I'm not confident the sofa springs will hold up.'

She could hardly breathe for anticipation as he strode down the landing with her in his arms. Opening a door at the end, he walked into a spacious room and kicked the door shut behind them. He carried her straight over to the bed and she barely had time to register that this was a very different room again: elegantly furnished in the Italian style rather than in the heavy traditional manner of the rest of the house. 'I like a man who knows what he wants.'

'And a woman who knows how to give it to him.'

She wouldn't argue with that, Holly thought as her breathing quickened. Ruiz's bed was big and firm, and had been recently dressed in crisp white linen. She was sure she could smell sunshine coming off the sheets. Lowering her onto the bed, he joined her and then, cupping her face, he kissed her. 'You're in a rush,' she said, fighting to catch her breath when he released her.

'Would you have me any other way?'

'Absolutely not,' she admitted. And then, because she was a glutton for punishment, she added, 'How about me?'

'Stop hiding behind the column,' Ruiz said frankly.

'And live a little?' Holly suggested.

'No.' He paused. 'Live a lot.'

Her body responded urgently as Ruiz kissed her again.

She loved the feel of his arms around her and the touch of him beneath her hands. She loved the taste of him and the smell of him, warm, clean and musky with rampant maleness. 'I'm so glad you invited me.'

'Don't play prim with me.' His lips tugged in a grin. 'I know what you want.'

'Seriously, Ruiz.'

'Seriously?' he queried, stopping her with a kiss. 'I know what you want. And you should know by now that I'll call you any way I have to, as loudly as I have to, from as far away as I must.'

She wasn't used to this feeling, this safe, sure, happy feeling. Maybe Ruiz was right and this was living. It was certainly risking everything for one man. And it was better this way. She stared into the dark amused eyes and knew then that for her this was the only way.

'Now stop trying to kid yourself and me,' Ruiz told her in a husky voice. 'We both know you're a very bad girl. So, what's holding you back, Holly?'

'Nothing,' she said, moving down the bed.

She took her time tracing the lines of Ruiz's muscular thighs. Then, pulling up his top, she traced the band of muscles across his belly. As her fingers trailed lower she had the satisfaction of hearing him suck in a fast breath. 'Was the belt really necessary,' she murmured. Cupping the arrogant swell of Ruiz's erection over the fabric of his jeans, she directed a teasing stare into his face. 'Is all this for me? You shouldn't have.'

Holly gasped out as Ruiz swung her underneath him. 'But I have and I will,' he promised as he began unbuttoning her shirt. 'And if you can't give me a very good reason for keeping me waiting for this, I shall just have to pleasure it out of you.'

'Oh, no. Please don't do that,' she murmured, watching

as Ruiz reached back to tug his top over his head. Tracing the formidable muscles on his chest, she turned her attention to his jeans. 'You are massively overdressed,' she complained, wrestling them off him. And massively erect, she discovered with excitement.

'And you are as forward as I remember.' Ruiz paid her back by whipping her top off and tossing it away.

'Lie on that bed, *Señor*,' she warned, stripping down to bra and pants. 'There is some unfinished business requiring my immediate attention, and it cannot wait.'

'Go easy, *señorita*,' Ruiz growled. 'I've been waiting a long time for this.'

'Are you saying the renowned playboy has lost his self-control?' she taunted, kneeling over him.

'I'm saying that with you it might be impossible to hold on.'

'Don't touch,' she warned when Ruiz reached for her breasts. Currently threatening to spill over her bra, her nipples were deep rose pink and erect.

'Do your worst,' Ruiz encouraged in a husky Latin whisper.

'Don't worry, I will,' she promised, slipping her fingertips beneath the waistband of his boxers. It was Holly's turn to suck in a fast, excited breath when she had removed them. Ruiz was magnificent in every department and most especially in this. She dipped her head to take him in her mouth, relishing his smoothness and the sheer size of him as she traced the veined surface with her tongue. She tasted and suckled gently, before licking him while cupping him with her hands. She wanted to hold him now, to feel the promise of pleasure beneath her hands. She needed both her hands.

'That's enough,' he exclaimed suddenly, swinging her beneath him.

'Can't you hold on?' she challenged him.

Ruiz's eyes were equally wicked. 'Let's find out, shall we?' he teased.

'Oh, yes. Let's,' she agreed with enthusiasm as Ruiz lost no time removing her remaining clothes. Nudging her legs apart with one powerful thigh, he tested and positioned her, using a pillow to raise her hips to an even more receptive level. After protecting them, he eased inside her with infinite care.

'That feels so good.' She breathed out a shuddering sigh as Ruiz lifted her.

'And now you can see,' he said.

She hummed, pretending that didn't matter to her. But it did. And now Ruiz had started to move his hips from side to side, so skilfully massaging he stole the breath from her lungs. Would it ever be possible to breathe normally again, she wondered, while Ruiz was inside her and stretching her so incredibly?

'This feels so good...' he said as he continued to roll his hips.

The pleasure was incredible and she gasped when he combined the massage he was giving her at the end of each stroke with a deep and steady movement back and forth. What made it even better was the way he withdrew completely each time, only to repeat the action again and again, until who would lose control first was no longer in doubt. 'Keep your legs wide,' he said, helping her to do so by placing the palms of his hands flat against the inside of her thighs and pressing them apart. 'I want you to do nothing, think nothing. All you have to do is feel, Holly, feel me...'

All she had to do was accept this steady pulse of pleasure growing inside her, while Ruiz worked to a dependable rhythm. A soft wail escaped her throat as the tension began to build to an unsustainable level. She tried to lie still as Ruiz had told her, but she couldn't blank her mind to what he was doing to her and knew it couldn't be long now... Perhaps one stroke, perhaps two—

He was ready for her, and when the strength of her climax threw Holly into his arms, he held her firmly as she bucked against him lost in pleasure. This felt so right. She felt perfect. Cradling her in his arms, he stared deep into her eyes to watch the fire rage and subside again into a series of pleasurable waves, each of which brought a groan of contentment from her lips. 'I think you liked that,' he murmured. His mouth tugged in a grin as he dropped a kiss on her parted lips. 'I think you liked that a lot...'

'I did,' she confirmed groggily. 'But now you have to keep that standard up.'

'You know I have very high standards.'

'And there's only one way to maintain them,' she murmured.

When he queried this with a raised brow, she murmured again, 'Regular practice.'

'Then I can only be grateful I rescued you from the samba club when I did.'

'You never told me how you knew.'

'Gabe called me at the gym,' he confided in a whisper against her mouth. He was already hungry for her again.

'Of course,' she whispered. 'So, what did he say, exactly?'

'He said that the pretty little thing he'd seen me with at the club was having trouble with some men.'

'Pretty little thing?' Holly queried, pulling back her head to stare at him. 'Are you sure he was talking about me?'

'Size is a matter of scale, isn't it?' he said, smiling

against her mouth. 'Or in your case, Holly, it's all in your mind.' He lavished an appreciative look down the length of her naked body.

She stretched extravagantly, no longer self-conscious or inhibited. 'You are rather large,' she said. 'I might hang onto you to keep me looking small.'

He laughed. 'You do that. Now, have I answered all your questions? Or would you like to talk some more?'

'Talk? No. Talking can wait,' she said, reaching for him. 'Don't be selfish,' she complained when he teased her by pulling away. 'You can't show off goods like that and then deny me the pleasure of them.'

'Again?' he said. 'So soon? Are you sure?'

'It's been at least thirty seconds,' she observed impatiently.

'Well, if I must,' he agreed, moving over her.

Ruiz was incredible. Big and hard and muscular didn't begin to describe him. Dangerously dark, with a wicked sense of humour, but even that didn't begin to scratch the surface of a man who meant so much to her. She was head over heels in love with him—in over her head—and it felt so good. There could be no half measures with a man like Ruiz, Holly reasoned gratefully as he probed and stretched and stretched her some more. 'I'm glad you came to my rescue at the club,' she managed to gasp before he took her mind off conversation. 'And now you can come to my rescue again.' Arching against him, she seized him with her muscles.

'Whoah, tiger,' Ruiz husked, responding just as she had planned. 'That's very forward of you.'

'Don't pretend you don't like it,' she said grasping him again. 'I know you better than that.'

He brushed her swollen lips with his, and then dipped his head to suckle her nipples as he thrust firmly into her. She sucked in a noisy breath. Nothing could have prepared her for this level of sensation. 'Brute,' she complained, balling her fists against his chest when he proceeded to ride her with the same easy control he used on his polo ponies.

'You love it,' he said confidently, maintaining the rhythm she adored. Cupping her face in his hands, he kissed her as he made love to her, and when he pulled away she thought that seeing her responses mirrored in Ruiz's eyes was the most erotic experience she had ever had. And now his kisses had grown deep and tender. 'I want you,' he murmured.

'I want you too.' He had no idea how much.

Burying his face in her breasts, Ruiz drew on her scent as she eased back her legs to give him greater access. Pressing her knees back, he brought her to the edge again. 'Now?' he teased her.

'Please,' she begged him, and only moments later she was bucking out of control with only Ruiz's firm hands to guide her and keep her safe.

'That was so, so good,' she murmured a long time later.

Kissing the soft swell of her belly, he moved on to Holly's heavy breasts to show them the appreciation they deserved. From there he kissed his way down the silky length of her body until he could bear no more, and, turning her on top of him, suggested she ride him.

'I'm not sure I've got your excellent technique,' she said.

She looked sultry and hot in the mellow light of early evening. Her red gold hair, burnished in the last rays of the sun, tumbled in glorious disarray over her breasts. 'Enough with the excuses,' he murmured, starting to guide her hips with his hands. 'Remember, practice makes perfect. This is almost as easy as the samba. That had three steps. This has two, forward and back…

'Who knew you'd be such an able pupil?' Ruiz commented with appreciation after a few minutes of this.

'At a guess?' she said. 'You.'

He groaned with contentment as she picked up the rhythm. It wasn't as if she hadn't made love with this man before, but being in control like this, directing his pleasure, took her feelings to a new level. She loved being in control. She loved teasing him by making him wait. She loved to see the tension growing in him as she brought him to the brink, though she couldn't keep him hovering there as he had kept her hovering, because she wanted to fall so badly too—

They fell together in a bucking, thrusting tangle of limbs as the pleasure waves hit them. She knew nothing more after that for a long while, and, as a slave to sensation, she was glad to be lost. When she woke she was still safely wrapped in Ruiz's arms. Their legs were tangled around each other and his sensuous face was relaxed. Thinking he must be asleep, she took hold of his hand to kiss each sensitive fingertip in turn.

'I trust you're satisfied,' he murmured.

'For now,' she agreed sleepily, turning her face towards him on the pillow.

'You'll exhaust me,' Ruiz complained, but his lips were already tugging in a wicked smile.

'I'm going to do my best to,' Holly agreed, 'though I think I still have some way to go,' she observed, registering the pressure of Ruiz's erection against her belly growing more insistent by the second.

Lifting himself up on one elbow, Ruiz smiled against her mouth. 'More?' he murmured, teasing her.

'Much, much more,' she agreed.

But first he caressed her with all the care and tenderness she had always dreamed of. Emotion wedded to strong sexual attraction was a wonderful thing, Holly had discovered, and Ruiz's stamina had never been in doubt. She exclaimed with the anticipation of pleasure as he turned her, touched her and entered her. She was on her side with her back to him, her legs drawn up in what was at once the most comfortable, as well as the most receptive position. She arched her back, offering herself for pleasure, while Ruiz held her and rocked her until the excitement became too much for her to bear.

Would he ever get enough of Holly? It seemed not, and it was torture holding back. She had no idea how much he wanted her or how deeply he had come to care for her. He hadn't realised that himself until he'd seen her here in Argentina. He had hoped she would accept his invitation, but he'd played it cool, played it down, because he had wanted this to be Holly's decision. He'd left airline tickets—a long shot based on nothing more than his belief that Holly had the same gut feeling he did that there was more ahead of them. The proof that he had been right to bring her to Argentina had blazed from her eyes the moment he'd seen her after the polo match.

Something vital had changed between them, Holly thought as Ruiz caressed her face. She hadn't been imagining things before; they were bound on more than a purely physical level. Breath shivered out of her in a soft moan as he cupped her buttocks in his warm, strong hands. 'You can't help yourself, can you?' she murmured, gratefully positioning herself.

'Maybe not, but I can help you.'

She drew back her knees to encourage him as he eased inside her. 'You're always so gentle with me,' she said.

'Until you tell me otherwise,' Ruiz agreed, 'and even then I'll be gentle with you.'

'Not even a little bit rough?' she said, provoking him as she wrapped her legs tightly around his waist.

'Fast and deep and hard is as rough as I'm prepared to get with you—'

'Get rough, then,' she said, smiling wickedly as she egged him on.

They made love for hours. Whenever Holly was briefly sated Ruiz coaxed her back into a state of arousal until she clung to him, rocked with him, moaning rhythmically as he coaxed her on to yet another welcome release. Not that she needed much coaxing. And when at last she did fall asleep for any length of time he kissed her and lay watching over her, knowing that he had never felt like this before. His feelings for her beat against his brain. They had never been in doubt, but what exercised his mind was how to make it possible for them to be together. Because they were going to be together. He was going to make it happen.

Rolling onto his back, he stared at the ceiling to think about his dual life in Argentina and London. And then there was his loyalty to the Band of Brothers. The London house he so badly wanted to make into a family home, the family *estancia* and the pampas he loved. And that was before he even got started on his horses and the polo—his whole crazy life. How could he ask Holly to share that when she was so gifted and career-oriented? He couldn't expect her to trot along meekly at his heels.

*Like Bouncer?*

He couldn't even be in the right place at the right time for the dog, let alone Holly. Come and live with me and fit in? Was that what he was saying? Try to shoehorn your life into mine—or into whatever small space I can spare for you? He had nothing to offer Holly. Throwing himself back on the pillows, he knew he would never ask so much of someone he loved. So what then? How could he keep her? And he must. They belonged together.

By giving her all the freedom she could want. By letting her go. By allowing Holly to make her own decisions.

*Dios!* That wasn't satisfactory. He was accustomed to being in control.

*He was accustomed to being alone. Did he want her or not?*

He had to wake her.

'What?' she murmured groggily as he kissed her awake. Reaching for him she was trusting like a child. She touched him tenderly, her fingers trailing down his arm, her eyes seeking reassurance in his. He wanted this. He wanted it for ever and not just for now. He wanted this closeness, this tenderness, this caring for each other, for ever and for always.

She smiled slowly. 'So you're still here,' she said.

'Of course I'm still here,' he confirmed, frowning as if anything else were inconceivable to him. And it was. It already was. It was unthinkable that he should be anywhere other than with Holly. The French called it a *coup de foudre*—a thunderbolt to the heart. He just knew it as love.

Ruiz introduced her to his brothers. They were dangerously good fun and ridiculously good-looking. Only Nacho remained a little reserved, but Holly felt his approval. 'You're good for my brother,' Nacho told her after supper that evening. 'I've never seen him so relaxed.'

Holly glanced at Ruiz, exchanging a look with him

that told her how pleased he was she fitted in and liked his family.

Fitted in for now, Holly mused the next morning after another spectacular night of love-making with Ruiz. Soon she would have to go back to London and return to work. Before then she had an article to write, but, though she sat and stared at the screen in the room Ruiz had set aside for her, the page remained resolutely blank. She turned with surprise when Ruiz walked in, managing to look sexier than ever in his knee-length riding boots, form-hugging breeches and tight-fitting top. 'Aren't you supposed to be training?' she queried.

'I changed my mind,' he said. 'It's no fun on my own.' Walking up to the computer, he typed in: FUN. 'That's what you need more of, Holly.'

'Didn't I have enough fun last night?' She rested her chin on her hand to stare up at him.

'That was then and this is now,' Ruiz argued. 'When I first met you Holly Valiant, you embraced fun. You couldn't get enough of it.' Putting his arm around her shoulders, Ruiz emphasised this comment with a kiss that made it hard to remember work. Holly stared down at the powerful forearm currently resting against her chest, all deliciously nut brown and muscular, and shaded with just the right amount of dark hair...

'Holly,' Ruiz warned softly, swinging her chair round so she had to look at him. 'You have to stop doubting me.'

'How do you always know what I'm thinking?'

'I just know you,' he said.

'So, why *are* you with me, Ruiz?' She searched his eyes.

'Let me think,' Ruiz murmured dryly. 'Could it be because I love you? Have you thought of that? Or are you just too frightened to put love in the frame in case you get hurt again?'

'Frightened? No.' She certainly wasn't frightened of Ruiz. She trusted him. 'You love me?' she said as if her brain had only just computed it.

'I love you, Holly Valiant,' Ruiz said, staring into her eyes.

'You can't say that just because we had good sex.'

'Surely you mean amazing sex?'

'Naturally, that's what I meant to say,' Holly agreed, adopting the same teasing tone. 'But that doesn't mean you love me,' she said, turning serious again. 'How can you be so sure of your feelings?'

'We've got plenty of time on our hands if you want me to prove it to you now.'

'Ruiz, please be serious—'

'I have never been more serious in my life,' he said, losing the smile. Taking both her hands in his, he stared into her eyes and then he kissed each of her hands in turn. 'I know you've been hurt in the past, but I will never hurt you, Holly. I want to be with you and to care for you always. If you'll have me…?'

For that split second she thought Ruiz looked as vulnerable as she felt. 'Who wouldn't want you?' she said. 'Not that I'm giving you licence to find out.'

'The only licence I want is one with both our names on it,' Ruiz assured her.

'Cheesy, but it might just work,' Holly said, starting to smile. This was happening. This was really happening. Holly Valiant had a boyfriend. And he loved her.

'It will work,' Ruiz said with confidence. Drawing her into his arms, he stroked Holly's hair back from her face. 'When will you go public with this?'

'In the column?' She gave him a cheeky look. 'You'll just have to wait and see—'

'This isn't for the column,' Ruiz said, turning suddenly serious. 'I'm asking you to marry me, Holly.' As he waited for her to say something he felt as if he were balanced on the tip of a mountain peak on one foot. 'I want to be with you, and I don't want anyone else,' he said. 'I want to share everything I have and everything I am with you, and I don't want to waste another second of our lives debating this. I want our future to begin now— here—right this minute,' he declared fiercely. 'I'm asking you to be my wife, but to be your own person too.' He stopped, knowing Holly's answer would be final, and that nothing in his life had meant this much to him before.

'Your life is so wildly different from mine,' she said, managing to smile and frown all at the same time.

'Wild is about right,' he agreed. 'But isn't taking chances what life is all about? There never will come a point where things are easy and straightforward, but if we can work through the challenges together we can make this work. And hopefully, there are some problems you wouldn't want to be without.'

'Like you?' she suggested.

'I'd rather think of myself as a challenge,' he teased her.

'I agree. Life would be boring without challenges, but endless problems are depressing.'

'Then let's not make a problem out of this. Do you accept my challenge?'

'I do,' she said.

'I love you, Holly Valiant.' He folded her in his arms.

'You love me?'

'I love you.'

'You love me,' Holly repeated, as if testing the words and finding them, not only plausible, but gradually, slowly, oh, so slowly, believable. 'You love me.' This time she smiled as she looked at him.

'Yes, I do,' he confirmed. '*Dios* send an angel to help me convince you,' he muttered beneath his passionate Latin breath. 'And if it takes a lifetime to prove it to you, then that is what I will do, Holly Valiant. So,' he said, 'having got the main challenge out in the open and sorted out, have you worked out yet what the missing link is where your writing is concerned?'

'I only wish I could,' Holly admitted worriedly, raking her hair with frustration. Her mind was so scattered, she could hardly concentrate. He loved her?

*Focus, Valiant, focus!*

'Let's take a shower.'

'Together?' she said, frowning.

'Is there any other way?'

'Your writing will be fine now,' he said later when they were both standing in front of the silent computer. 'Before, you had just shut your mind to anything that frightened you, stifling original thought.'

'And I suppose you've just done me a favour in the bedroom by opening it up again?'

'It certainly helped,' he said. 'I think I can give you some further help if you need it,' he added, glancing at the sofa.

'Don't you think of anything else?'

'With you around?' His lips pressed down. 'Rarely.' Grabbing her hand, he pulled her across the room. 'I bet I can give that imagination of yours a real kick-start.'

'I'll try anything once,' Holly said, gamely.

'Excellent. First play and then work—'

'If you think that's the solution,' she said, 'We'd better get to it.'

'I couldn't have put it better myself. I think you're going to write the best article of your life after this, Holly Valiant, and then I'm going to teach you to ride.'

She laughed. 'And after that?' she queried.

'After that we're going to show everyone how to dance the samba—'

'You're completely mad,' she exclaimed as he lowered her down onto the cushions.

'Mad for you,' Ruiz agreed, unfastening his belt.

# CHAPTER TWELVE

WHEN Holly was lying quiet and contented in Ruiz's arms, she asked him, 'Did you mean it?'

'Did I mean what?' he said, opening one wicked eye.

'You know,' she prompted.

'Say it, Holly.' Ruiz raised a brow as he waited.

'When you said…you love me.'

'Of course I did—I do.'

With a hum she settled back in his arms again. 'I'm glad you didn't go riding right away.'

'Oh, so am I,' Ruiz agreed in a mocking tone and with a smile Holly didn't see. 'But I am going to try out a new horse in a while, so you'll have plenty of chance to write your article.'

'Slave driver.'

'Don't tell me I haven't filled you with enough inspiration yet?' Dipping his head, Ruiz stared with laughing eyes into Holly's sated gaze. He knew this was the only way they could both be happy—if he let her be free to explore her talent and her career.

'You've certainly given me enough to go on for now,' she said, reluctantly staggering a little as she got to her feet and walked to the desk.

'Just call me back if you need any more help,' he said, springing up and adjusting his clothing.

'Don't worry, I will,' she said, already logging on.

Being singled out by Holly meant more to him than she could ever know. He was so used to being one of the Band of Brothers: Ruiz, the youngest, the fixer, the travelling glue pot for the family. The man who made things right again. He was so busy sorting things out he had never stayed anywhere long enough to form a lasting attachment, let alone with someone as precious to him as Holly. And now he wanted to do something special for her. She had to know how much he cared about her, how much he loved her. It was almost Christmas, and Christmas Day was also her birthday. Gifts for his brothers were easy—anything for their horses. Lucia was almost as easy. He could take his sister on a virtual shopping trip and let her choose anything she liked, but he didn't want to do that with Holly. He wanted to choose something that had meaning for her. He wanted to spoil her because she had never been spoiled, and surprise her because he loved to see her laugh.

She had bought Christmas presents for the Acosta family, knowing she would be staying over the holidays with them, but she couldn't find the perfect gift for Ruiz, the man who had everything—or who could buy it in the unlikely event he found a gap.

She had an idea. She'd have to work on it, and she'd have to work fast, Holly concluded, pressing Send on her latest 'Living with a Playboy' feature, along with a second message marked 'URGENT'. The main article for *ROCK!* was still work in progress, and something told her that unless she wrote a couple of alternative endings she would have to wait until after Christmas to complete the final draft of that.

'Are you ready for your riding lesson?'

She turned as Ruiz entered the room. 'As I'll ever be!'

'Not chickening out, I hope?' he said, smacking a whip against the side of his sexy, calf-moulding riding boots.

'You wish,' she said.

'No, I'll leave that to the pony,' Ruiz said, laughing. 'Come on.' Throwing an arm around her shoulders, he led her out of the room.

Ruiz put her up on a young, dark bay gelding called Dulce. 'Can I have hand rails?' Holly asked nervously, feeling she should have a safety harness at the very least.

'Hang onto me,' Ruiz suggested, springing onto the back of a waiting stallion. 'Dulce is very light on the mouth, but he'll be kind to you. Squeeze your knees together and he'll go forward.'

'Not sure I can squeeze my knees together...'

Ruiz laughed. 'Then do the best you can.'

'Well, I blame you if I can't get them to move together.' But, experimenting, she discovered her knees still worked. She found the small horse remarkably biddable too, and with Ruiz at her side, patiently advising her, she also discovered confidence flooding in. 'I like it,' she exclaimed with surprise, urging the kind pony to pick up his stride.

'Do you like him?' Ruiz asked when she had successfully completed a couple of circuits of the ring.

'I love him,' Holly admitted, stroking the pricked, velvety ears as she rested her cheek against Dulce's firm, warm neck.

'He's yours.'

'What?' She sat up. 'You can't do that.'

'Who said I can't? Happy Christmas, Holly.'

'But when will I be able to ride him?'

'Whenever you come to Argentina with me.'

'Are you serious? Who will ride him in the meantime?'

'The grooms will ride him. What will it take to convince you?' Ruiz demanded, riding alongside. 'Shall I call my brothers over and ask them to convince you that I never joke where horses are concerned?'

'Don't do that,' she said, flashing a glance at the posse of impossibly tough-looking bad boys busy training fresh young ponies in the next paddock. 'I've got more than enough trouble on my hands as it is. So,' she said, narrowing her eyes as she stared at Ruiz. 'If you never joke about horses, how about women?'

'There are no women.' Ruiz gave her a long, intense stare. 'There's only you.'

'Good, because I tweeted our news resulting in a mega uplift in hits to the site.'

'Oh, I'm delighted,' Ruiz said dryly.

'A love story contained in one hundred and forty characters isn't bad editing.'

'Not bad at all,' Ruiz agreed. 'You should think about taking up writing as a career...' He dodged out of the way as she aimed a swipe at him.

'So if we're going to be together do you think I should kill the column?' she said.

'Of course not,' Ruiz argued.

'You don't think the readers will grow bored now they know the outcome?' Holly said, frowning.

'I'm disappointed in you, Holly. What has happened to that imagination of yours? There should be at least three spin-offs from this piece of news.'

Would that be the engagement, the wedding, followed swiftly by the first baby? Holly wondered.

Ruiz swiftly disillusioned her. 'Cleaning his tack, ironing his shirts, and cooking the playboy's meals should do it.'

'You mentioned dancing?' she said as he helped her to dismount.

'Yes. We're having a party at the *estancia* this evening.'

Holly hummed. 'I'd watch your toes if I were you.'

The Christmas Eve celebration was being held in the main courtyard and, dressed in jeans with her hair piled up high, Holly had pitched in with the staff to help them dress the walls and balustrades with garlands of flowers to augment the colourful blossom in the garden. The cobbled area was lit by candlelight and torches held in high brackets on the walls, and there was a full moon that cast a spotlight on the glittering fountains. The band was already playing sexy South American music and there were professional dancers on hand to demonstrate the various styles of dance to the guests, as well as enough food and wine to feed an army. The banquet had been set out on trestle tables dressed with crisp white linen, boasting silver cutlery and twinkling crystal. Holly was just about to go and get changed when the biggest surprise of the night waylaid her. Lucia had arrived under cover of darkness to surprise her brothers. The two girls had been in touch by e-mail in order to spring a few more surprises before the night was out.

'It's just like the old days at school,' Lucia commented, handing over Holly's Christmas present. 'All this subterfuge, with the added amazingness of you and my brother falling in love—' Lucia broke off to give Holly the biggest hug ever. 'Come on, sister-to-be, let's go and get changed. You can hardly arrive at the party wearing jeans.'

The outfit Lucia had chosen for Holly was spectacular. The slinky dress in vivid red had a low vee neck and the highest of high hemlines. Lucia had also chosen a pair of silver sandals with stratospheric heels to wear with it.

'You look fabulous,' Lucia exclaimed when they had sneaked into Holly's bedroom and locked the door securely behind them. 'Now get those sandals on,' she prompted. 'If Ruiz loved you before, his tongue will be sweeping the floor when he sees you wearing this...'

'I'd rather Ruiz kept his tongue in his mouth,' Holly remarked dryly, turning her head to examine her back view in the full-length mirror.

'The answer is no,' Lucia assured her. 'It doesn't look big. It looks perfect. You look perfect.'

'And you shouldn't be spending so much money on me.'

'And you weren't supposed to pay me any rent,' Lucia countered. 'I couldn't believe it when I saw the amount you put into my bank account.'

'The column is going well.'

'That doesn't matter. Whoever gave you my bank details is so dead!'

'Take the money. I can afford to pay you the going rate,' Holly reminded her best friend. And didn't that feel good. 'You look pretty fabulous for a change,' she added wryly, staring with renewed interest at her beautiful friend. 'What's the special occasion, Lucia?'

'Only pretty fabulous?' Lucia said worriedly, examining her back view in the same mirror.

'You know you look as gorgeous as you always do,' Holly volunteered. 'But you still haven't told me what the special occasion is...'

'Why does it have to be special? It's just a family party.'

'And you are making a very special effort,' Holly noted as Lucia checked her make-up in the mirror.

'Okay, so I hear Nero Caracas is bringing his polo team as well as his new wife and baby tonight,' Lucia explained off-handedly. 'Which means Luke Forster, that American polo player, will be at the party. Don't look like that, Holly. Luke's far too stern and serious for me. And he's about ten feet tall.'

'Poor man,' Holly murmured, remembering she had seen the good-looking American commanding the field of play quite a few times during the game.

'But I might enjoy teasing him,' Lucia added thoughtfully as she arranged her ample breasts in the low-cut dress.

'Excellent news for Luke,' Holly agreed tongue in cheek. 'So are you ready to spring our surprise?'

Ruiz, meanwhile, was pacing up and down his bedroom with the phone gripped so tightly in his hand it was threatening to break apart. 'What do you mean you couldn't arrange it? I told you well in advance what I wanted. Plus there's an agreement between our two countries so there shouldn't have been a problem. What has happened to the vet? How can he have left on another flight when I booked him? I booked the jet, damn it!' Ruiz thundered. 'Who the hell countermanded my order?' Ruiz whirled around as one of his brothers poked his head round the door. He waved him away. Business was all-important, and when it was business concerning Holly nothing came before that.

'Are you coming to the party, Ruiz?' his brother Diego asked him, refusing to be so easily dismissed.

'When I'm ready,' he snapped.

'Would you like me to look after Holly for you?'

His answer to that was to lob a polo ball at the door, which his brother dodged. 'Only asking,' Diego murmured, closing the door.

So his surprise for Holly was ruined, Ruiz raged inwardly. Lucky for him the jeweller in Buenos Aires hadn't let him down. Checking the breast pocket of his jacket, he decided he'd better go down to the party, but he was nowhere near ready to give up on his other surprise for her yet.

Holly and Lucia had barely walked into the party when three of the Acosta brothers spotted their sister and came straight over. Their reunion was touching and Holly envied their closeness. This wasn't the constant squabbling and petty jealousies Lucia had described at school. It was the deep and abiding affection of people who knew everything there was to know about each other, and made Holly long for her own family.

With all the constant squabbling and petty jealousies that might involve, she thought with amusement as Lucia batted the most formidable of her brothers, Nacho, on the head with her frivolous party purse. 'How dare you summon me back like an employee, you great oaf? And what have you done with Ruiz?' Lucia demanded, swinging round. 'Holly has a special surprise for him and he's not even here. Don't tell me you've sent him back to London to work?'

Nacho huffed dismissively. 'I can't tell your brother Ruiz what to do.'

'Quite right,' Lucia agreed dryly. 'Ruiz is too busy telling me what to do.'

As Lucia kissed each of her brothers in turn Holly

grew increasingly anxious. Was her surprise for Ruiz going to fall flat?

'Last time I saw Ruiz he was pacing his bedroom like a bear with a sore head,' Ruiz's brother Diego murmured discreetly in her ear. 'I'd give him a few minutes.'

'Thank you.' Holly smiled her thanks.

As the darkly glamorous men peeled away to welcome their guests other men were drawn like moths to the two girls standing on the edge of the dance floor. Holly was quite relieved to see the driver who had brought her from the airport amongst them. He bowed so politely over her hand she was only too delighted to accept. He was fun, she remembered, as her portly partner chuffed his moustache before leading her onto the dance floor. The dress Lucia had given her was really working its magic, Holly thought as she started dancing. She had never worn such a beautiful party dress before. She glanced gratefully at Lucia, noticing with amusement that Lucia had just walked straight up to the attractive American polo player, Luke Forster, only to veer away at the very last moment on the pretext of tugging one of her brothers onto the dance floor. It was also interesting to see Luke Forster's brooding amber gaze following Lucia as she sashayed off.

Holly had only been dancing with the driver for a few minutes when another man tapped the driver's shoulder and cut in. This man spoke no English, but he danced well and held Holly at arm's length so their bodies always had air between them. She was really enjoying herself, though still worrying about Ruiz and wondering where he could be. And then a younger man, who had clearly had too much to drink, decided it was his turn to take Holly on a drunken lurch around the floor. Unfortunately his grip was so secure she couldn't break free, and now Lucia was making frantic signals from the edge of the dance floor. Like a drama slowly unfolding that no one could stop, Holly saw Ruiz emerge from the house and stand at the top of the steps to scan the dance floor. The young man who had Holly in his grip decided that this was the perfect moment to launch his assault. Wet lips pursed, he darted his head forward, and as she whipped her head away to avoid him a big black shape launched itself on Holly and her partner, barking wildly as it knocked them to the floor.

'Bouncer?' Holly exclaimed, wiping muddy paw marks from her arm. She looked up to find Ruiz dressed in full evening rig standing over her. He looked more magnificent and formidable than she'd ever seen.

'No harm done,' Ruiz said in a tone Holly had never heard him use before as he brushed the man's suit down and called for one of the gauchos to escort him away. 'How the hell did Bouncer get here?' he demanded with frustration.

'Please don't be angry with Holly,' Lucia begged him, hanging onto her brother's arm.

Easing himself free, Ruiz took hold of Holly. 'Well?' he murmured.

Their faces were very close. Ruiz's mouth was almost touching hers. Everyone at the party was frozen to the spot, sensing drama. There was no music, no chatter, not a sound to be heard—until Bouncer whimpered and both Holly and Ruiz knelt simultaneously on the ground to make a fuss of him. As if this were the signal everyone had been waiting for the music started up again and the dance floor came back to life.

'Happy Christmas, Ruiz,' Holly murmured, staring across Bouncer's head into Ruiz's eyes. 'I think Bouncer had this planned from the first moment we met, though

Lucia brought him over in the private jet with the vet,' she explained, 'and as Bouncer has had all his shots and has a pet passport and Argentina has the same arrangement for allowing pets to travel as the EU...'

'This I know,' Ruiz assured Holly, softly holding her within an inch of his mouth as he lifted her to her feet. 'I do deal quite a lot with the authorities in both countries, you know? Shipping ponies?' Ruiz's lips tugged in his trademark smile. 'I tried to bring Bouncer over to surprise you for Christmas too, but it appears you beat me to it.'

His brothers, hearing this, congratulated Holly.

'Nice to know someone can get the better of you, Ruiz,' the great Nacho Acosta commented dryly before moving away to ensure the party didn't flag.

'I thought it would be better for Bouncer to live here on the pampas than in London,' Holly admitted. 'Your brothers agreed. But then I hesitated until Nacho said you had mentioned the same thing to him.'

'Nacho agreed to Bouncer coming to live here?" Ruiz demanded with surprise.

'He did more than that. Nacho arranged the jet,' Holly explained. 'He said it was a long journey for a rescue dog to take unaccompanied, but with Lucia and a vet on hand he thought it might be possible.'

*'Dios!'* Ruiz glanced at his brother who raised a glass.

'Are you pleased with your surprise?' Holly asked anxiously.

'I couldn't be more pleased,' Ruiz said, holding Holly a little closer as the dance floor filled up. 'But you've left me without the possibility of giving you a surprise.'

'Oh, I don't know,' she said. 'I can't believe we've exhausted your repertoire yet...'

Ruiz's wicked mouth tugged in a grin. 'So you don't need a surprise right here, right now?'

'In front of all these people? Absolutely not,' Holly murmured.

'What am I going to do with this, then?'

She stared at the small jewel box. 'What is it?'

'The next headline for your column,' Ruiz said dryly.

'If that's what I think it is.'

'It is,' Ruiz murmured, 'but I think you'd better get out of that dress first.'

Holly sucked in a breath, remembering only now that her dress was ruined and covered in mud.

'We have very good dry cleaners in Argentina,' Ruiz reassured her, slipping the jewel case back into his pocket.

'But I couldn't possibly let you pay the bill…'

Their faces were very close as both of them relived a day in London that seemed such a long time ago now.

'Shower?' Ruiz murmured with a very particular look in his eyes.

'As soon as possible,' Holly agreed.

'Ruiz and Holly. I like the sound of that,' Ruiz commented as they strolled back to the house together arm in arm.

'Holly and Ruiz,' Holly corrected him.

'I'll go for that,' Ruiz conceded. It was an easy victory for Holly. He was just quietly celebrating that the world and everything in it was his now, while Bouncer, who was safely back in Lucia's keeping, barked his satisfaction at a job well done.


'So what do you think, Holly?' Ruiz demanded as Holly stared in thrilled delight at the huge ruby on her wedding finger.

'I think you're a very dangerous man,' she said as Ruiz moved behind her.

'Have you only just noticed that?' Ruiz murmured against her neck.

As she turned in his arms Ruiz's gaze slipped to her lips. 'Stop it,' she warned him softly as he whispered a world of wickedness in her ear.

'No one will notice if we don't return to the party right away…'

Ruiz had a point. He also had a formidable erection. And as they were both standing naked beneath the shower she thought it rude not to seize the moment.

*It's big and red and fits me perfectly. Rubies are the perfect choice for a fiery redhead, Ruiz told me. You can know his name now, seeing as the playboy and the redhead are going to be headline news in the next issue of this magazine—front cover too. And the column?*

*This column will continue, for, as my polo-playing bad boy points out, I can send copy to ROCK! from anywhere in the world, and there should be plenty more headlines to come—especially as Ruiz has three gorgeous brothers and a baby sister, my best friend, Lucia. You can read all about them here— The Good, The Bad, and The—*

*Well, not ugly, since all of them are stunningly glamorous, lead the most riotous lives, and are the best fun to be around. You'll have to stay tuned to find out.*

*Hasta la vista! Here's to the next time we meet.*

\* \* \* \* \*

*Read on for a sneak preview of Carol Marinelli's*
PUTTING ALICE BACK TOGETHER!

Hugh hired bikes!

You know that saying: 'It's like riding a bike, you never forget'?

I'd never learnt in the first place.

I never got past training wheels.

'You've got limited upper-body strength?' He stopped and looked at me.

I had been explaining to him as I wobbled along and tried to stay up that I really had no centre of balance. I mean *really* had no centre of balance. And when we decided, fairly quickly, that a bike ride along the Yarra perhaps, after all, wasn't the best activity (he'd kept insisting I'd be fine once I was on, that you never forget), I threw in too my other disability. I told him about my limited upper-body strength, just in case he took me to an indoor rock-climbing centre next. I'd honestly forgotten he was a doctor, and he seemed worried, like I'd had a mini-stroke in the past or had mild cerebral palsy or something.

'God, Alice, I'm sorry—you should have said. What happened?'

And then I had had to tell him that it was a self-diagnosis. 'Well, I could never get up the ropes at the gym at school.' We were pushing our bikes back. 'I can't blow-dry the back of my hair...' He started laughing.

Not like Lisa who was laughing at me—he was just laughing and so was I. We got a full refund because we'd only been on our bikes ten minutes, but I hadn't failed. If anything, we were getting on better.

And better.

We went to St Kilda to the lovely bitty shops and I found these miniature Russian dolls. They were tiny, made of tin or something, the biggest no bigger than my thumbnail. Every time we opened them, there was another tiny one, and then another, all reds and yellows and greens.

They were divine.

We were facing each other, looking down at the palm of my hand, and our heads touched.

If I put my hand up now, I can feel where our heads touched.

I remember that moment.

I remember it a lot.

Our heads connected for a second and it was alchemic; it was as if our minds kissed hello.

I just have to touch my head, just there at the very spot and I can, whenever I want to, relive that moment.

So many times I do.

'Get them.' Hugh said, and I would have, except that little bit of tin cost more than a hundred dollars and, though that usually wouldn't have stopped me, I wasn't about to have my card declined in front of him.

I put them back.

'Nope.' I gave him a smile. 'Gotta stop the impulse

spending.'

We had lunch.

Out on the pavement and I can't remember what we ate, I just remember being happy. Actually, I can remember: I had Caesar salad because it was the lowest carb thing I could find. We drank water and I *do* remember not giving it a thought.

I was just thirsty.

And happy.

He went to the loo and I chatted to a girl at the next table, just chatted away. Hugh was gone for ages and I was glad I hadn't demanded Dan from the universe, because I would have been worried about how long he was taking.

Do I go on about the universe too much? I don't know, but what I do know is that something *was* looking out for me, helping me to be my best, not to **** this up as I usually do. You see, we walked on the beach, we went for another coffee and by that time it was evening and we went home and he gave me a present.

Those Russian dolls.

I held them in my palm, and it was the nicest thing he could have done for me.

They are absolutely my favourite thing and I've just stopped to look at them now. I've just stopped to take them apart and then put them all back together again and I can still feel the wonder I felt on that day.

He was the only man who had bought something for me, I mean something truly special. Something beautiful, something thoughtful, something just for me.

© Carol Marinelli 2012
Available at millsandboon.co.uk

*A sneaky peek at next month...*

# MODERN™

### INTERNATIONAL AFFAIRS, SEDUCTION & PASSION GUARANTEED

## *My wish list for next month's titles...*

**In stores from 17th February 2012:**

❏ Roccanti's Marriage Revenge – Lynne Graham

❏ Sheikh Without a Heart – Sandra Marton

❏ The Argentinian's Solace – Susan Stephens

❏ Girl on a Diamond Pedestal – Maisey Yates

**In stores from 2nd March 2012:**

❏ The Devil and Miss Jones – Kate Walker

❏ Savas's Wildcat – Anne McAllister

❏ A Wicked Persuasion – Catherine George

❏ The Theotokis Inheritance – Susanne James

❏ The Ex Who Hired Her – Kate Hardy

**Available at WHSmith, Tesco, Asda, Eason, Amazon and Apple**

## *Just can't wait?*

0212/0

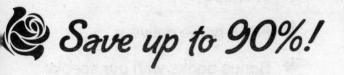

# MILLS & BOON® Book Club

## 2 Free Books!

## Get your free books now at
### www.millsandboon.co.uk/freebookoffer

---

## Or fill in the form below and post it back to us

**THE MILLS & BOON® BOOK CLUB™—HERE'S HOW IT WORKS:** Accepting your free books places you under no obligation to buy anything. You may keep the books and return the despatch note marked 'Cancel'. If we do not hear from you, about a month later we'll send you 4 brand-new stories from the Modern™ series priced at £3.30* each. There is no extra charge for post and packaging. You may cancel at any time, otherwise we will send you 4 stories a month which you may purchase or return to us—the choice is yours. *Terms and prices subject to change without notice. Offer valid in UK only. Applicants must be 18 or over. Offer expires 31st July 2012. **For full terms and conditions, please go to www.millsandboon.co.uk**

Mrs/Miss/Ms/Mr (please circle) _____

First Name _____

Surname _____

Address _____

_____

_____ Postcode _____

E-mail _____

Send this completed page to: Mills & Boon Book Club, Free Book Offer, FREEPOST NAT 10298, Richmond, Surrey, TW9 1BR

Find out more at
**www.millsandboon.co.uk/freebookoffer**

Visit us Online

0112/P2XEA